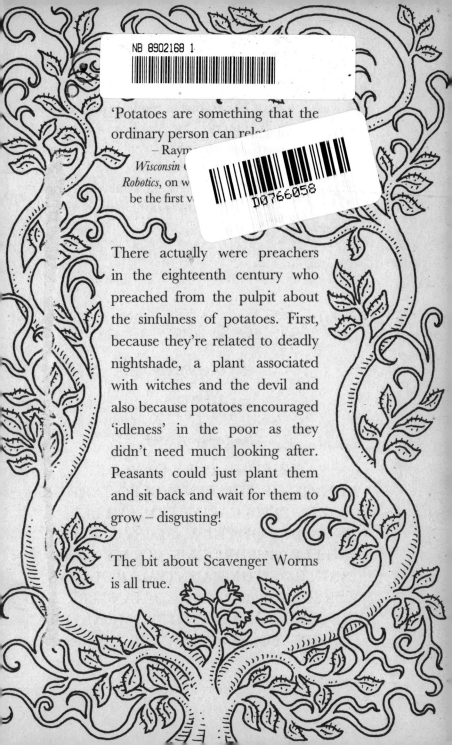

'Potatoes are something that the ordinary person can rel...
– Raym...
Wisconsin ...
Robotics, on w...
be the first v...

There actually were preachers in the eighteenth century who preached from the pulpit about the sinfulness of potatoes. First, because they're related to deadly nightshade, a plant associated with witches and the devil and also because potatoes encouraged 'idleness' in the poor as they didn't need much looking after. Peasants could just plant them and sit back and wait for them to grow – disgusting!

The bit about Scavenger Worms is all true.

Susan Gates was born in Grimsby. Her father is a guitar player and her mother was a tailoress. When she was at school her favourite reading was science fiction and she had a craze for American Literature, especially detective fiction. She went on to study American Literature at Warwick University. She then became a teacher and taught in Malawi, Africa. She has three children and lives in County Durham, England.

Books by Susan Gates

For Older Readers

DUSK

For Younger Readers

A BRIEF HISTORY OF SLIME!
ATTACK OF THE TENTACLED TERROR
DR FELL'S CABINET OF SMELLS
INVASION OF THE VAMPIRE SPIDERS
KILLER MUSHROOMS ATE MY GRAN
NIGHT OF THE HAUNTED TROUSERS
RETURN OF THE MAD MANGLER
REVENGE OF THE TOFFEE MONSTER
THE SPUD FROM OUTER SPACE

SUSAN GATES

THE SPUD FROM OUTER SPACE

ILLUSTRATED BY
TONY BLUNDELL

PUFFIN

PUFFIN BOOKS

Published by the Penguin Group
Penguin Books Ltd, 80 Strand, London WC2R 0RL, England
Penguin Group (USA), Inc., 375 Hudson Street, New York, New York 10014, USA
Penguin Books Australia Ltd, 250 Camberwell Road, Camberwell, Victoria 3124, Australia
Penguin Books Canada Ltd, 10 Alcorn Avenue, Toronto, Ontario, Canada M4V 3B2
Penguin Books India (P) Ltd, 11 Community Centre, Panchsheel Park, New Delhi – 110 017, India
Penguin Group (NZ), cnr Airborne and Rosedale Roads, Albany, Auckland 1310, New Zealand
Penguin Books (South Africa) (Pty) Ltd, 24 Sturdee Avenue, Rosebank 2196, South Africa

Penguin Books Ltd, Registered Offices: 80 Strand, London WC2R 0RL, England

www.penguin.com

First published 2004
1

Text copyright © Susan Gates, 2004
Illustrations copyright © Tony Blundell, 2004
All rights reserved

The moral right of the author and illustrator has been asserted

Set in 14/16.5 pt Monotype Baskerville
Typeset by Rowland Phototypesetting Ltd, Bury St Edmunds, Suffolk

Made and printed in England by Clays Ltd, St Ives plc

British Library Cataloguing in Publication Data
A CIP catalogue record for this book is available from the British Library

ISBN 0-141-31516-4

Chapter One

Cruncher was furious with his thumb.

'Behave yourself,' he raged at it.

He'd just woken up. And there it was again, plugged into his mouth like a dummy.

'Got to stop doing that,' Cruncher scolded it for the millionth time.

No one outside his family knew about it. But it was still deeply embarrassing. It was something babies did! When he got dozy, just before he went to sleep, that thumb slid into his mouth like a fat pink slug.

'You're sucking your thumb in all your baby photos,' Mum would say, while Cruncher cringed. 'You were so sweet.'

Cruncher wanted to stop. It was desperately urgent. Time was running out. He was grown-up now. He was going to secondary school in September.

Thumbsucking wasn't the only bad habit Cruncher wanted to break. Number two on his list was crisp eating. He was a crispoholic! He ate six, seven bags a day. He'd even got his nickname, Cruncher, because of his passion for crisp munching.

But not any old crisps would do. It had to be his favourite brand, Chapel Crisps. They were made in a little factory, converted from a church, near where Grandad lived. They were the best, the crackliest crisps ever. On the noise scale they scored ten out of ten. Ten and a half. No other crisps came near.

Cruncher never left home without several bags in his pockets. That was in case he couldn't get fresh supplies. Chapel Crisps were hard to find. The corner shop sold them. But he'd never seen them anywhere else. The lady loading the crisp shelves at Tesco's had shaken her head. 'No, we don't sell those, love. Never heard of 'em.'

Sometimes, Cruncher thought, *I'll never be able to leave this estate, ever.* Because, without his favourite crisps, he just couldn't survive.

But he had to cut down. His baggy pants had loads of pockets. But lugging a whole day's supply around in them was bad news. It made his trousers crackle when he walked. Made his body look bulgy in embarrassing places. And if he ever got to kiss any girls, they'd say, 'Gross. Your breath stinks of cheese-and-onion.'

Besides all that, eating so many crisps was seriously bad for his health.

He had six weeks to shape up, make big changes. Secondary school was his chance for a fresh start. For a few seconds, Cruncher's face was grim with purpose.

Then he took a packet of Chapel Crisps from under his pillow. Not to eat. Just to look at.

Handmade, it said on the bag. Cruncher imagined a smiling, apple-cheeked old granny in a frilly pinny, dropping spud slices one by one into golden, spluttering fat. That's why Chapel Crisps tasted so good. They had the human touch. Each single crisp was made for kids, *lovingly*.

If he ever got to meet that old granny, Cruncher would shake her hand and say, 'You should get a medal.'

Cruncher had the crisp bag in his clutches. But he didn't pop it open.

'I've got the willpower!' he told himself, amazed.

It was his second favourite flavour, smoky bacon. He shook the bag. A rustling sound came from inside. It was as if the crisps were whispering to him, '*Crunch us.*'

Instantly, his willpower crumbled. He fell on the crisps like a starving wolf. In a wild attack, he ripped the bag open, held it above his mouth. Tipped the crisps in. *KERRUNCH*. What a salty explosion! Crisp crumbs sprayed everywhere. He blew the bag up like balloon. Smashed it between his palms. It burst, *BLAM*. Shreds of silver floated down to the carpet.

'*Ahhhhh.*' Cruncher gave a deep, contented sigh. That felt better.

He just loved everything about crisp scoffing. The whole noisy experience. From the first rattle of the crisp bag, to the last *BLAM* when he blew it up.

But then his happy smile scrunched into a frown. 'Failed again,' he scolded himself, like a stern teacher. Would he *never* be free of crisp munching and thumbsucking?

Cruncher scowled at his thumb. All his other fingertips and even his left-hand thumb had whorls on them. But his right-hand thumb was sucked smooth as a plum. If the police ever wanted to fingerprint it, there'd be nothing there.

That thumbnail's getting long, noticed Cruncher. He'd better cut it soon. He always kept it short, so he didn't stab himself when he thumbsucked in his sleep.

Wait a minute, he thought. He'd just had a dazzling idea. Wasn't he trying to get tough with himself? Why snip his thumbnail at all?

Let it grow really long, he told himself eagerly. *Then sharpen it, like a dagger. Then you can't thumbsuck, can you? Cos if you try, you'll stab yourself to death and* die.

'Yeah,' cried Cruncher, punching the air. At last, he'd found a solution to thumb-sucking. A kill or cure method. He felt really cheered up.

That's thumbsucking sorted, he thought.

He just had his crisp problem to deal with now.

Chapter Two

Three weeks later.

'How beautiful,' sighed Cruncher. Grandad was standing beside him. They were staring up into the night sky.

The sky's like a dark-blue carpet, thought Cruncher, dreamily. *Sprinkled with diamonds.*

'Look,' he cried out loud. 'There's a shooting star! I'm gonna make a wish.'

'Don't bother,' said Grandad. 'That's no shooting star. That's just a piece of space junk, burning up in Earth's atmosphere.'

Cruncher's magical, fairy-tale mood was whisked away. He caught a whiff of stinking rubbish. And remembered where he was. He was at the council tip.

The landfill site, where bin lorries growled in and out, was shut. The clanking JCBs that buried the garbage were silent. Even the sea-gulls, who whirled about all day in shrieking clouds, were still.

One part of the tip was still open though. It was the bit Grandad ruled over, where people came to dump their household rubbish.

Cruncher looked down on Grandad's Little Kingdom – the skips, the caravan where Grandad lived, the big garage-sized shed that was always locked. The little shed with its huge antennae and satellite dishes where Grandad tracked space junk . . .

Oh no, Cruncher was thinking. Grandad was getting all fired up about his favourite subject. Grandad's life was rubbish – he was interested in anything about it, especially when it was out in space.

'Not content with mucking up this planet,' Grandad was ranting on, 'we've started on space now! Do you know how many pieces of man-made junk are whizzing about up there? From old space missions and exploding satellites?'

'Millions, Grandad,' answered Cruncher, automatically.

While Grandad raved about space junk,

Cruncher was thinking about something else, something much more fascinating.

'And future generations can forget about space exploration,' Grandad was fuming. 'They won't get 300 kilometres before their rocket gets ripped apart by a screwdriver going ten times faster than a rifle bullet. And another thing –'

'Grandad,' Cruncher chipped in, 'how do spacemen go to the toilet?'

Grandad glared down at his grandson. He was a big bloke, like a great, shambling bear. His bushy eyebrows became one stern line.

'Kids should be interested,' said Grandad, 'in major environmental issues like garbage disposal.'

'Yeah, well I am,' said Cruncher. 'Honest. But it's just that I've always wondered –'

'It's not *how* they go,' said Grandad. 'It's what they do with it afterwards. More human waste to dispose of. But *worms* are the answer.'

'Pardon?' said Cruncher,

'Worms,' repeated Grandad, as if it was obvious. 'Worms in space.'

Then, suddenly, just when Cruncher was getting interested, Grandad fell silent. He was staring out over the council tip.

What's he seen? thought Cruncher, trying to follow his gaze.

Grandad's Little Kingdom was lit up in a cosy, yellow glow. People were still driving in, dumping bin bags of garden rubbish into the skips. But the massive landfill site where Grandad was looking was eerie and dark. It was like a moonscape, with craters, even seas. Big lagoons, on the far side, shimmered silver in the moonlight. They were full of potato sludge, the waste product from the Chapel Crisps factory.

Cruncher could see the warning signs from here. DANGER. DEEP SLUDGE LAGOONS, they said. KEEP OUT.

He could see the crisp factory too, beyond the high wire fence snagged with fluttering carrier bags. From the outside, it still looked like an old church. It even had stained-glass windows. Without that CHAPEL CRISPS sign above the door you'd never guess what was going on inside.

But Grandad was pointing into the dark heart of the landfill site.

'Can you see anything?' he asked Cruncher. 'By that big JCB?'

Cruncher strained his eyes. There was a

muddle of moonlight and shadows. Then, in the blackest patch, he thought he saw a light. It was very feeble. Was it moving? It flickered, like a firefly. Then went out.

'I saw *something*,' said Cruncher.

Grandad looked troubled. 'It was her, wasn't it? The Little Waif, I call her. That poor ragged child who roams over the tip.'

Cruncher said, 'Eh?' His face creased up in confusion. 'I never saw a ragged child. I thought I saw a light, that's all. But it's gone now.'

Grandad shuddered, as if he was shaking off a bad dream.

'You're right,' he said to Cruncher. 'There's nothing there.'

Except for, buried deep beneath the garbage mountains, the ruins of a village called Robin's Corner. Grandad didn't even bother to mention that. Everyone round here knew the story of Robin's Corner. How there'd been a great fire, 300 years ago, that had destroyed the village. Burned all the houses like dry sticks. Almost no one had escaped.

'Anyway,' said Cruncher, trying to get Grandad back to more important matters. 'What about these worms?'

'Worms?' said Grandad, looking vague.

'You said they took *worms* up in space rockets.'

'I didn't say that. They haven't actually *done* it yet. It's still in the planning stage. They've hit a big snag.'

'But *why*?' asked Cruncher, desperately. '*Why* do they need worms in space?'

'They're special Scavenger Worms. They'll eat anything. But they're particularly partial to human waste products.'

'You mean they eat –'

'Exactly,' Grandad interrupted. 'And then the Scavenger Worms pass it through *their* digestive system. And it comes out as compost – that spacemen can grow vegetables in. Isn't that neat?'

'Wait a minute,' cried Cruncher, his mind boggling. 'Are you telling me spacemen eat vegetables grown in their own poo? They don't do that on *Star Trek*. That's disgusting.'

'It's highly efficient recycling,' corrected Grandad. 'And, remember, worms ate it first. So it's Scavenger Worm poo, technically.'

'I still don't want my tomatoes grown in it! Come on, you're kidding me, aren't you, Grandad?'

'I'm not,' said Grandad, looking offended. Grandad never joked about waste disposal. 'I'm being deadly serious. On long space flights people will need fresh food to keep them healthy. But, like I said before, there's a snag with these Scavenger Worms.'

Cruncher thought, *Do I really want to know?* But it was no good, he had to ask.

'What snag?' he said.

But Grandad was busy checking his watch. 'Is that the time? I've got to close up.'

Grandad forgot about worms in space. Gave one last thought to the ghostly Little Waif he'd seen several times now, scrambling up the mountains of rotting rubbish.

The first time, he hadn't been sure what he was looking at. He'd seen a blurry shape, like a smudged drawing, with light rippling gently round it. He'd rubbed his eyes and it was gone.

But the second time, she was clearer.

Surely, he'd thought, horrified, *that's not a child on the tip scavenging for food? That doesn't happen, does it? Not here. Not nowadays. Her feet are bare. She's got no shoes!*

He told himself, *You should call the police. Call social services.*

He'd unlocked the big gates with his personal keys, gone charging in.

Those mountains could slide and shift, burying you in putrid waste. And what if she fell into a potato lagoon?

'Hey,' he'd shouted. 'Little girl! You shouldn't be in here. It's not safe.'

He could still see her, shining feebly in the distance, like a white moth flitting about on a garbage heap.

He'd staggered, gasping, to where he'd seen her. There was nothing there. He'd stared round at the rubbish mountains.

Silly old fool, he'd told himself. *You need your eyes testing.*

But he'd felt the hairs at the back of his neck wriggling, like maggots.

Cruncher was tugging at his sleeve. 'Grandad? Grandad? You said you'd got to close up.'

Chapter Three

The last people had driven off from Grandad's Little Kingdom. They'd just dumped a rabbit hutch in a skip.

'That's a perfectly good rabbit hutch,' said Grandad, taking it out again.

'Someone will want that,' he told Cruncher.

Grandad had a little business on the side, selling things he'd salvaged from the skips. It always amazed him, what people threw away. Not just rabbit hutches. But computers and tellies.

'That's not rubbish. It's not even broken,' Grandad would say, bewildered.

Even if it was broken, Grandad could usually fix it, or take it apart and make it into something else. He was a genius at recycling. He'd made most of his space-junk tracking equipment that way – from stuff other people chucked out.

Cruncher sometimes wondered, *Is there* anything *he can't recycle?*

Grandad padlocked the gates to his Little Kingdom, put up the CLOSED sign.

He and Cruncher walked back, past the big shed, the one Cruncher had never been allowed in. For the hundredth time, Cruncher asked, 'What are you hiding in there, Grandad? Go on, tell me.'

Grandad tapped his nose and said, 'Top secret.'

He always said that. Cruncher usually tapped his nose and said 'Top secret' with him. But just in time, he remembered his thumb.

He thought, *That could've been nasty.*

His right-hand thumbnail was now a deadly weapon. Long and dagger-sharp. He loved that nail. He'd be heartbroken if it snapped.

With its help, he'd bust his thumbsucking habit. He'd had a few accidents, just when he was dozing off. Slid his thumb into his mouth, shish-kebabbed his own tongue. But he'd soon learned not to do that.

You had to be careful though. Like just now. He could have ended up with a third nostril. Or when you were gelling your hair, for instance. That dagger thumbnail could poke your eye out.

But that was a small price to pay. He'd cracked that babyish habit. He'd never suck his thumb again. Not ever.

'Just got to check something!' cried Grandad, interrupting Cruncher's thoughts. Grandad dashed into his little shed, the one that bristled with antennae and satellite dishes.

Cruncher crackled after him. He'd solved his thumbsucking problem. But he'd made hardly any progress with the crisps – he'd got ten packets of Chapel Crisps concealed in his trousers. He was staying overnight with Grandad. So he needed a good supply.

Cruncher slumped into a rickety deckchair that Grandad had rescued from a skip.

His bum sagged nearly to the floor. *Crackle, crackle. Whoops*, he thought. *I'm crushing my crisps.*

Better eat them. He found the crushed packet in his back pocket. He slashed at the bag. *Rrrip*. That dagger nail wasn't only an anti-thumbsucking device. It was also dead useful for popping crisp bags.

Cruncher munched away. Good job he had crisps to pass the time. Watching Grandad track space junk was boring.

When Grandad started building his radar system, Cruncher couldn't wait for it to be finished. He was really excited.

There was all kinds of stuff up there! Tiny nuts and bolts, car-sized fuel tanks. Even an astronaut's glove, lost during a space walk – it was whizzing round the Earth at 28,000 kilometres an hour.

'The fastest and most deadly glove in history,' Grandad had told Cruncher, gravely.

Sometimes, the junk got snatched by gravity and slowly spun back down to Earth. Mostly it burned up in Earth's atmosphere. But now and again it didn't. Grandad had told him a story:

'In Uganda, one night, there was a thunderous noise. *Boom!* A flash of light, a wave of scorching heat. A woman went running out of her house. And a booster from an old space rocket had landed in her maize field. Made this massive crater.'

'*Wow,*' said Cruncher. 'Do you think any

space junk will land here?'

Grandad shook his head. 'No use hoping for miracles.'

And when the radar system was up and running, Cruncher felt even more disappointed. It was a big let-down.

There'd be a little *Ping!* like a microwave telling you your chips were done. Then Grandad would rush to the screen. 'Look, that's probably a piece of space junk!'

'It's just a little green blip, Grandad,' Cruncher would protest, 'that goes *ping*.'

But now Grandad was talking as if something exciting was really happening. He was showing Cruncher the screen.

'Look, there it is – I've been tracking it for days. I couldn't believe it at first. It's getting closer every day.'

Cruncher perked up. This was more like it. 'So it *is* going to land here?'

Grandad shook his head. 'The odds are zillions to one against it. It could end up in Mexico. Or Outer Mongolia.'

Same old, same old, Cruncher thought, munching ten crisps at once. Space junk never came here. It always went somewhere else, or burned up like a shooting star.

'There's money in space junk retrieval,' said Grandad, suddenly. 'Big money.'

'Yeah?' said Cruncher, sitting up and paying attention.

'Whoever designs a spacecraft to clean it up will be a billionaire. Something like one of our bin vans,' explained Grandad, trying to make it simple. 'Except with a few little adjustments. Course, you'd need to give the bin crews a bit of extra training –'

'A *bit* of extra training?' Cruncher butted in. 'Grandad, astronauts don't put out wheelie bins! Collecting space junk is totally different from collecting it round the streets!'

'In some ways it's very similar,' said Grandad, looking stubborn. 'Did you know there are bin bags in space? The Russian space station Mir released 200 of them, filled with rubbish.'

'But, Grandad, down here rubbish stays still. In space it's whizzing past you at 100,000 kilometres an hour.'

'That's why I said the bin van will need a few little adjustments.'

Cruncher gave up. It was no use arguing with Grandad when he was in this mood. You could never win. He shook his head sadly. Bin vans in space? It was just one of Grandad's crazy dreams. Like space junk landing right outside his back door. It would never happen.

There was a knock on the shed door.

Who's that? thought Cruncher. Grandad's Little Kingdom was a friendly place. Bin men and women from the council tip were always calling in for a cup of tea and a chat. But not this time of night.

A guy in a greasy white lab coat came bursting through the door. 'Just on my way to the sludge lagoons. Can I borrow your spare set of keys?'

'Cruncher,' said Grandad, 'meet Professor Lester Kettles, the owner of Chapel Crisps. The Prof is the world's top potato scientist. What this chap doesn't know about spuds isn't worth knowing.'

Chapter Four

Cruncher couldn't believe it.

He was actually looking at the man who made his favourite crisps. The crisps he was trying to cut down on – but just couldn't, because they were so tasty, so crunchy, so wonderfully noisy . . .

He suddenly sprang forwards. 'Without your crisps my life wouldn't be worth living!'

He grabbed the Professor's hand, pumped it up and down. 'You're my hero,' he confessed.

'*Ow!*' cried Prof Kettles. He gazed in bewilderment at the bead of blood on his palm.

'Sorry, sorry,' said Cruncher, shoving his dagger thumb out of sight in his pocket.

Professor Kettles didn't look like anybody's hero. He was tall and weedy with floppy yellow hair that fell over his face in curtains.

He looked like an Afghan hound. Except he had popping green eyes that any frog would be proud of. He had a flower in his buttonhole: a tiny blue and crimson one. It was a potato flower, of course. Potatoes were his passion. To him they were the most wonderful vegetables. Far more fascinating than, say, carrots or turnips.

'Sorry,' said Cruncher again, deeply embarrassed that he'd wounded his hero.

But the Prof had already forgotten the pain. His gooseberry eyes fizzed with enthusiasm.

'So you're a fan of my crisps?'

'Yes!' said Cruncher. 'Listen to this.' He stretched out his arms, shook his body like a belly dancer.

'I'd know that crackle anywhere,' said Professor Kettles.

Cruncher was really impressed. 'You mean, you can tell your own crisps by their crackle?'

'Of course,' said Prof Kettles. 'The crackle quotient is really important in crisp manufacture.'

'Eh?' said Cruncher.

Grandad butted in, 'The Prof is interested in the science of crisps. He's a boffin,' he added, as if that explained everything.

'The *science* of crisps?' said Cruncher, baffled.

'Well, I first started out studying potatoes,' said Prof Kettles. 'But then crisps became my special interest. Did you know, each time we crunch a crisp we break open the air-filled cells inside it, making that high frequency sound which we call "crackly"? That's why Chapel Crisps are especially noisy,' said Prof Kettles proudly, 'because they have such a high crackle quotient. A high crackle quotient is the key to the perfect crisp.'

High frequency sound? thought Cruncher. *Crackle quotient? Why is he being so complicated?*

'When I crunch a Chapel Crisp,' said Cruncher, 'I feel like – like a caveman!'

'Pardon?' said the Professor.

'Yeah,' said Cruncher. Suddenly, he felt truly inspired. Words came tumbling out of his mouth.

'What's the first thing you do with a bag of crisps?' he asked Prof Kettles.

'Well, I would calculate the crackle quotient. For Chapel Crisps, for instance,' the Prof said, 'it's 87.3 per cent. Not perfect. But we're getting there.'

'No, no, no!' said Cruncher, hopping about

with frustration. 'Kids don't calculate crackle quotients.'

'Kids?' said Professor Kettles, looking blank.

'Yes, kids. They're the ones who mostly buy crisps.'

But the Prof never thought about marketing. He only thought about crisps from a scientific point of view. That's why he didn't sell many. Cruncher was probably his best customer.

'Anyway,' said Cruncher, 'first thing a kid does is tear open the bag. No, rip it open,' he corrected himself, his dagger thumb twitching in his pocket.

Cruncher got out a bag to demonstrate. 'See, *RRRIP*. There's the bag busting open. Then you grab the crisps, cram them in your mouth. *KERRUNCH*. You smash 'em,' he said, chomping madly, 'like a caveman crunching a woolly mammoth bone. Then you blow up the bag. *BLAM*. You explode it. And then you feel like this . . .'

Cruncher beat his skinny chest, gorilla style. 'CAVEMAN!' he roared, ferociously.

Professor Kettles shrank back, alarmed.

But Cruncher hadn't finished yet.

He gave another savage roar, just to make sure they'd got the point. '*GRRR!*'

Grandad and the Prof were staring at him open-mouthed. Cruncher thought, *What are they looking at me like that for?*

He slumped back into the deckchair, totally exhausted. It was hard work being brilliant. He'd known for a long time that crunching crisps gave him a big boost. But he'd never put it into words before. Never thought, *That's the caveman feeling.*

Grandad said, 'Have you gone stark raving mad?'

But to Cruncher's relief the Prof leapt in to defend him. 'No, this is fascinating. Tell me, do only Chapel Crisps have this effect?'

'Course,' cried Cruncher. 'Cos they're the noisiest, the crunchiest crisps in the universe.'

Grandad shook his head as if to say, 'I haven't got a clue what you two are talking about.'

But Prof Kettles and Cruncher smiled at each other. It was a meeting of minds. Cruncher had found another crisp fanatic. Someone who took crisps even more seriously than he did.

'Would you like a tour round my factory?' asked the Professor.

'What, you mean right *now*?' said Cruncher.

'Why not?' said the Prof. 'I've just got to dump some potato sludge first.'

'Wow. Can I, Grandad? Can I?' asked Cruncher.

But Grandad didn't answer. His eyes were locked on to his radar screen again. Up in space, junk was whizzing silently round like great shoals of fish in a vast, dark sea.

The bit Grandad was tracking had separated itself from the others. It was on a journey of its own. A lone piece of space junk, in low Earth orbit.

'*Hmmm*. Wonder what it is?' Grandad murmured.

He would probably never know. Most likely, it would burn up before it landed.

Cruncher had no time for little green blips. The most thrilling event of his life was about to take place. He was going on a tour of Chapel Crisps. He couldn't wait.

'Keys, keys, Grandad,' said Cruncher, clicking his fingers. '*Ow*.' He must remember not to do that, now he'd made his thumbnail a deadly weapon.

Grandad handed over his spare keys, without taking his eyes off the screen. 'Careful with those. There are the keys to my Little Kingdom and the council tip on that keyring.'

'Bye!' cried Cruncher, crackling out of the door after the tall, swooping figure of Professor Kettles.

Left alone in his shed, Grandad shivered. His radar screen cast an eerie green glow on his face. He couldn't shake off the sinister feeling that the Little Waif and this piece of junk spinning closer to Earth were somehow connected. She'd appeared the same night he'd noticed it on his radar screen. And, as it got nearer, she seemed to get less ghostly, more like flesh and blood.

Grandad shook his head. 'Silly old fool. It's just a coincidence. Besides, that little girl isn't there. It's your eyes playing tricks.' Moonbeams, chasing each other over the garbage mountains, could confuse you.

'Cruncher didn't see her,' he reminded himself. And Cruncher had much sharper eyes than he did.

'Climb in,' Professor Kettles told Cruncher.

There was a battered old tanker parked outside Grandad's shed. It was full of potato sludge, a gloopy soup of peelings and bruised bits of potato, the waste products from the crisp factory. The tanker had a long, flexible tube for pumping the sludge into the potato lagoons. It couldn't be pumped into rivers – it poisoned the water, killed all the fish.

'*Phew,*' said Cruncher, holding his nose. 'This stuff pongs like blocked drains.'

'Wait until you get to the potato lagoons,' said the Prof cheerily, starting up the engine. 'Some people pass out from the smell.'

Professor Kettles drove out of Grandad's Little Kingdom to the great metal gates of the council tip. They were topped with rolls of barbed wire, to stop people climbing in.

While the Prof got out to unlock them, Cruncher stared into the tip. He'd never been in there at night, only a couple of times during the day, when friendly bin crews had given him a ride in their cabs.

They drove into the tip. The Prof leapt out again. Cruncher heard the great gates clanging shut behind the tanker. The sound made him shiver. For some reason he thought, *Like the Gates of Doom.*

That thumb was sliding out of his pocket, like it sometimes did in moments of stress.

'No way!' Cruncher told it fiercely. How embarrassing, if his hero saw him thumb-sucking, like a baby.

I'd never live it down, thought Cruncher. And besides, he didn't want to spear his own tongue with that spiky nail. There'd be blood all over the place.

Instead, he took a bag of Chapel Crisps out of his baggy pants. *Slash, rip.* He attacked the packet in a frenzy. Using his left hand, he stuffed his mouth full. *KERRUNCH*. Crisp fragments shot everywhere like shrapnel. He mashed those crisps to a soggy mess. Total demolition. No mercy.

'Caveman!' growled Cruncher, thumping his chest, Tarzan style.

'*Ouch.*' His dagger thumb scratched his ribs, through his T-shirt.

But he sneered at the pain. He felt big and tough. As if he could wrestle a sabre-toothed tiger.

It would be even harder to give up crisps now. *Just one more little mouthful*, thought Cruncher.

The sound exploded inside his head,

CHOMP, as the rest of the crisps were mangled.

With a fierce look on his face, Cruncher blew up the bag. Burst it with his dagger thumb. *POW*. The bag hung in tatters. The crisps were annihilated. There was nothing left to destroy.

'*Ahhhh.*' Cruncher sank back in the seat.

There was a happy grin on his face. Being a caveman, just for a few seconds, made him feel like he could face anything.

He glanced behind him. *Why had those big metal gates looked so menacing?*

'Gates of Doom?' He shook his head. 'Cruncher, that's *so* pathetic.'

The Prof got back into the cab. The tanker's headlamps threw a white beam of light in front of them. It showed the dirt track that led to the potato sludge lagoons. The Prof started driving along it. In seconds, dark rubbish mountains loomed all around them.

'I'm President of Spud Buddies,' the Professor chatted away to Cruncher. 'We're a small group of fans who want to tell the world that potatoes are *really groovy*. We've got our own web site.'

'Oh yeah?' said Cruncher, trying to look

interested. 'How many people visit your web site?'

'Three,' said Professor Kettles.

'What, only three a day?'

'Three a year actually,' admitted the Prof. 'And we don't have many young members. That's a worry.'

'Do you have *any*?' asked Cruncher, amazed.

'*Er*, no,' the Prof confessed. 'But kids will soon be queuing up to join Spud Buddies. I've made our web site much more kid-friendly. I've included a list of exciting books about potatoes. Most of them are by me,' the Professor said, modestly. 'And a photo of the World's Most Famous Potato.'

'The World's Most Famous Potato?' repeated Cruncher, baffled.

'Yes,' raved the Prof, as they jolted between garbage mountains. 'I think kids will love it. They can print out the photo if they like. Pin it up on their bedroom walls.'

Cruncher sniggered. He tried not to. But he just couldn't stop himself.

He'd seen a famous potato once. A kid had brought it to school. It was shaped like something really rude. Cruncher thought, *Shall I tell*

Professor Kettles about it? But somehow, he guessed that the Prof wouldn't share the joke.

Professor Kettles sighed. Most people sniggered when he talked about his lifelong passion. Some even fell about laughing. He couldn't understand it. What was so funny about potatoes?

Cruncher stifled his sniggers. He tried to ask an intelligent question. 'So what is this potato famous for then? The one you've put on your web site.'

'For being the first potato in space,' said the Prof. 'In fact, this spud was actually grown out in space, on the American space shuttle *Columbia*, to be exact.'

Awful connections were being made in Cruncher's brain.

But Professor Kettles was rambling on. He had two dreams in life. One was to make the perfect crisp. And the other was to share the wonder of spuds with the world.

'People think potatoes are just lumpy, boring vegetables.' He laughed in disbelief at this. 'They're very rude about them. They call each other couch potato, potato head. That's really insulting – to potatoes!'

Cruncher wasn't listening. He was still

thinking about that Space Potato. What did they grow it in? Weren't worms to compost astronaut poo still in the planning stage? Hadn't they hit a big snag? He could have sworn Grandad had told him that.

Cruncher was already feeling queasy. He thought, *Do I really need to know this?* But he just had to ask: 'So did they have Scavenger Worms on this space shuttle?'

Professor Kettles suddenly braked hard. Cruncher was thrown against his seat belt: 'Hey!'

But the Prof had already jumped out. He was running round the tanker, peering beneath it. Cruncher thought, *Has he hit something?*

After a long time searching, the Professor climbed slowly back in.

'I thought I saw . . .' He rubbed his eyes. 'I could have sworn . . .' His voice trailed away. He switched off the tanker's engine.

They sat in silence.

Dark, sinister mountains towered over them. Cruncher shivered. You wouldn't know Grandad's cosy Little Kingdom was so near. It felt like they were stranded on an alien, unfriendly planet, in some remote galaxy.

Then he remembered something else. But that only made it even more spooky. Deep beneath them were the ruins of Robin's Corner, the tragic village that was burned to cinders.

The fire was started by a wicked girl called Jane Shore – so the old story said. There was even a little rhyme about her.

> *Jane Shore, Jane Shore,*
> *The wicked wretch, she must be found,*
> *Let loose the biggest hound!*
> *Jane Shore, Jane Shore,*
> *She burns houses to the ground.*
> *Hunt her down! Hunt her down!*

After what she did, no wonder everyone hated her. No wonder they wanted to hunt her down with dogs.

Cruncher scolded himself, *What are you thinking about her for?* He hadn't thought about her for years.

'Why are we waiting?' he asked the Professor.

Prof Kettles didn't reply. He was just staring ahead, as if he'd been hypnotized.

'Professor?' said Cruncher. His own voice almost scared him. It sounded so loud and echoing in the silence. 'Is something the matter?'

Suddenly there was a gust of wind from somewhere. A torn black plastic bag fluttered across in front of the tanker, like a bat.

It seemed to snap the Professor out of his trance. He shook his head, started up the engine. The headlamps' beam blazed out again, lighting up the darkness, showing them the way ahead.

'This place is scary at night,' said Cruncher, as they drove on. Those garbage mountains, so dark and brooding; the tragic village buried beneath them. He crunched a few crisps – tried to get back that caveman feeling.

'Dumping this sludge won't take long,' said the Professor. 'Then it's off to see some hi-tech crisp production.'

He seemed his usual bouncy, spud-crazy self. But his green eyes were troubled. He'd seen a child, on the track, right in front of the tanker. He'd only got a glimpse before he slammed on the brakes. She was gaunt, hollow-eyed. Her ragged clothes were scorched, as if she'd been too close to a fire. And she was holding her hands out, as if begging for food.

He felt sure he'd braked too late, that she was under the wheels. His heart had almost stopped with horror. But when he'd jumped out to check, there was no little girl. Not under the tanker or anywhere else. He'd searched all around, while the cold, silver moon looked down on him. There was no child anywhere.

Professor Kettles was shocked but not surprised. He'd seen other things lately, at the crisp factory. At first, when he'd moved in, everything had gone smoothly. His crisp production line had run without a hitch. But just lately there'd been strange noises, disturbances, creeping shapes in shadowy corners. And often, he'd whipped his head round, convinced he was being watched. And found nobody there.

He was sure there was a scientific explanation. He just hadn't found it yet.

One of the potato lagoons was filled to the brim. It looked like a quaking bog, with a thick crust of green cheesy mould growing on top. The Prof headed for the one that was half empty. Pulled up beside the sign that shrieked DANGER at you in big, red letters.

'*Phew*,' said Cruncher. He covered his nose, taking care not to shove his dagger thumb up his nostril. 'You were right about the pong. It's disgusting.' It made the stink of rotting rubbish seem like perfume.

'It's the putrefying potatoes,' said the Prof. 'I quite like it.' He took a big deep lungful. '*Ahhh.*'

He climbed out and hauled the long, flexible pipe over the edge of the lagoon. The potato slurry came slurping out, like sloppy porridge.

'Don't fall in,' said Cruncher anxiously out of the tanker window.

'Better not,' said Professor Kettles. 'Potato sludge is like quicksand. The more you struggle, the more it sucks you in.'

He needn't sound so cheery about it, thought Cruncher, shuddering.

If he hadn't had that spiky nail, his thumb might have sneaked towards his mouth. But he'd given that up for good. Instead, he reached for another crisp bag.

Hope he hurries up, thought Cruncher, munching madly.

'*Caveman,*' he chanted. But it was just a whisper.

This place was giving him the creeps. He couldn't wait to get to Chapel Crisps. His

crisp supply was down to six packets. Maybe he could wangle a few free samples.

From the top of a dark garbage mountain, the Little Waif watched them.

Her body wasn't hazy and transparent. She was growing more solid by the hour. You could make out details. See her big, hungry eyes, the dark patches under them like black-berry stains. See her grimy bare feet, blue with cold.

And even see, if you looked hard enough, on her right hand, a long, spiky dagger-shaped thumbnail.

Down in his Little Kingdom, Grandad couldn't believe his eyes.

'It's going to pass right overhead!' he said, staring at the little green blip.

Grandad snatched his telescope. Went dashing outside.

Might be lucky, he thought. He might even be able to see it, a tiny fireball, as it whizzed through the heavens. On its way to land who knows where? Maybe in the Atlantic Ocean.

He searched the night sky. But he didn't even need his telescope. There was the space junk. Still miles away, trailing flames behind it. But it wasn't whizzing past. It was plunging earthwards, right over the council tip.

'It's landing here,' breathed Grandad. It seemed incredible. But somehow, he was certain of it. 'It is! My very own piece of space junk.'

It was a zillion to one chance.

Grandad didn't know it yet. But chance had nothing to do with it. The space junk was coming here for a purpose. It had an appointment to keep.

Chapter Five

'Welcome to Chapel Crisps.' Professor Kettles waved Cruncher in.

His voice seemed as bright and chirpy as ever. But his goggly green eyes flicked anxiously round the factory, checking the darkest corners for anything suspicious.

'It's just your imagination,' he told himself. 'Get a grip.'

Nothing must get in the way of his mission: to use his potato knowledge to make the perfect crisp.

No one understood potatoes like he did. Spuds had always been special to him. He'd had a lonely childhood. His parents had owned a fish and chip shop. They'd been far too busy frying to pay him any attention. He'd spent hours in the kitchen of the chip shop, with only potatoes for company. To most people, all spuds look the same. But little Lester had made potatoes his friends. He'd given them names, talked to them, could tell them apart. His parents could never understand his howls of distress when they'd taken away his potato chums to make them into chips.

'Wow,' said Cruncher, staring round the factory.

He hadn't expected anything like this.

One or two things reminded you it had once been a church. The stained-glass windows were still there. So was the high, wooden pulpit, in one corner, where the preacher climbed to give his sermons. But everything else had been ripped out and replaced with hi-tech crisp-making machinery. Cruncher saw a long conveyor belt and a huge, stainless steel tank for frying, big enough to fit a car in. A great silver chimney rose up into the roof, to take the fumes and smell away.

'Course, it's all worked by computer,' explained the Professor. 'The whole factory practically runs itself. It doesn't need people.'

Cruncher's visions of an apple-cheeked old granny lovingly frying each single crisp went right out of the window.

He felt a bit cheated. 'But it says on the bag that Chapel Crisps are made by hand.'

'It doesn't say *human* hand though, does it?'

Prof Kettles went swooping over to a computer. Cruncher tried to follow: '*Whoops!*' He slid on a grease slick, nearly went flying.

The Prof shook his head in sympathy. 'You just can't get rid of the grease. However hard you try. I wear shoes with specially grippy soles.'

Cruncher skated over to join him.

'Want to see it all working?' asked the Prof. Cruncher nodded eagerly.

'You'll have to wear one of these,' said Professor Kettles, 'for hygiene reasons.'

'It's a hairnet!' said Cruncher, appalled. 'A pink one! No way!'

But the Prof was already tucking his floppy blond locks into his hairnet.

'Oh, well,' shrugged Cruncher – so long as none of his mates was here to see him. He tugged his hairnet on, trying not to snag it with his dagger thumb.

'Right,' said Professor Kettles. 'Here goes.' He punched a button marked 'Power', tapped some computer keys.

The conveyor belt started rumbling.

Potatoes were joggling along it towards the fryer. From the great silver tank came the greasy reek of hot fat.

'Before,' the Prof was saying, 'you needed loads of different machines. One for sorting the potatoes, one for peeling, one for slicing –'

Zzzz. Cruncher felt himself dozing off. How could crisp making be so boring? Had he put on a hairnet for *this*?

'But I've got a machine that does it all in one go,' said Professor Kettles, his froggy eyes shining with enthusiasm. 'It's a revolution in crisp making.'

The Prof stood close to the conveyor belt and, in a loud, clear voice commanded, 'LET'S MAKE CRISPS.'

Cruncher thought, *Why's he speaking with an American accent?*

There was a whirring sound. Cruncher saw something rise up slowly at the end of the conveyor belt. It glittered in the light. At first Cruncher was dazzled. 'What is it?'

It turned, with another whirring sound. Then Cruncher saw. It was a silver fist, with the fingers folded. Like a metal gauntlet from a medieval knight's suit of armour.

Whirr. One by one, the fist flexed its fingers.

43

They were many-jointed, like lobsters' legs. And each one was tipped with a long, sharp talon.

'Meet Claw,' said Professor Kettles, in his own normal voice.

Cruncher shivered. Claw looked brutal. As if it should be wielding a two-headed axe in some savage battle. Not making fun, bubble-filled snack foods in a crisp factory.

But the Prof didn't seem to find Claw strange or sinister. He was like a kid with a new toy.

'Just watch Claw in action!' he said.

The conveyor belt carried the jiggling potatoes closer. Claw shot out. It wasn't free to move on its own. It was fixed to the floor, on a long, extendable arm. Like lightning, it picked through the potatoes. Pushed some off the belt.

'They're the bruised ones,' said Professor Kettles. 'Only perfect spuds go to make Chapel Crisps.'

Cruncher watched, stunned, as Claw gripped each potato. *Zippp*, ripped its skin off in one curling ribbon. *Whop, whop, whop*. They were sliced with those deadly talons. None escaped. Paper thin, see-through slices, each one exactly the same thickness. Then Claw scooped up the slices. Dumped them into the silver tank. *Sssss!* The fat hissed and sizzled. Claw waited. For five seconds. Then plunged into the boiling oil after them.

Cruncher gasped. 'It'll fry!'

'Don't worry,' said the Prof. 'It's made of special metal. It can stand very high temperatures. It's practically indestructible.'

Claw scooped the crisps out, spitting and crackling, shook them once, twice. Flung them on to a wire rack to cool.

'LET'S TAKE A BREAK,' Professor Kettles commanded, talking American again.

Whirrr. Instantly, the silver hand obeyed. Claw bunched up its fingers, its job done. It waited for the Prof to give it its next orders.

'Wow,' said Cruncher, shivering. 'That Claw's a beast.'

'It's a robot,' corrected Professor Kettles, striding towards the freshly fried crisps. 'Programmed to obey simple voice commands.'

'Why do you have to talk to it in American?'

'It won't recognize my English accent,' said the Prof. 'It was made in the USA.'

Cruncher skidded after him as if he was on an ice slide.

45

The Professor tested a crisp. He didn't crunch it. He just snapped it, right next to his ear. His eyes closed, as if he was listening to beautiful music. He snapped it again.

'A crackle quotient of 88.8!' he announced, looking pleased. 'The best yet. Try one.'

Cruncher didn't need asking twice. He didn't test for crackle quotient. He just put his mouth on a level with the cooling rack and shovelled in as many crisps as he could. His cheeks bulged like a hamster. His jaws scissored. The *KERRUNCH* was earth-shattering. It echoed inside his skull.

You caveman, Cruncher told himself. This time he remembered his dagger thumb and didn't thump his chest.

'Claw would like to meet you,' said Professor Kettles. 'Go and say hello.'

'Wot?' said Cruncher, through a mouthful of mashed crisps.

'Go and say hello,' repeated the Prof.

'You sure?' said Cruncher. He slithered over to the metal fist. His pink hairnet was too big. It kept sliding over his eyes. He pushed it up so he could see. Claw was resting now. But it still looked menacing.

'Hello, Claw,' said Cruncher warily.

The robot hand stayed motionless.

'It doesn't want to say hello,' said Cruncher, relieved.

'LET'S MEET AND GREET,' cried the Professor.

Claw's talons suddenly shot out. Pointed at Cruncher like a wizard casting a spell. Then came snaking towards him.

'*Aaaaargh!*' cried Cruncher, staggering backwards.

But Claw couldn't reach him. It was yanked back, like a dog on its chain, by that long, flexible arm that was bolted to the floor.

'Don't be scared,' chuckled the Prof. 'It wants to shake hands.'

'No way,' said Cruncher. What if it peeled, sliced and fried his fingers? Made them into crisps?

'It's only being friendly,' the Prof assured him.

Cruncher took a few steps forwards. Instantly, Claw seized his hand in its iron grip. Trapped his soft, pink fingers in a metal cage.

'Get it off me!' yelled Cruncher. 'It'll crush my fingers!'

'It won't,' said the Professor. 'It can cradle a fluffy newborn chick without hurting it. It can do embroidery. It's very sensitive.'

And sure enough, Cruncher felt his own hand gently waggled up and down by those silver talons.

'Cool,' he said. But his voice was shaky. His legs felt like jelly.

What was it doing now? Cruncher squirmed, but he daren't snatch his hand away. Those cruel talons were crawling all over it, brushing his skin, as lightly as spiders' legs.

'*Yurgh*. It's tickling.'

'It's only scanning your hand,' said Professor Kettles. 'Learning your hand shape. So it knows you again.'

Did Claw linger, when its talon tips brushed Cruncher's dagger thumb? As if, for the first time, it had found something like itself? Another Claw?

Cruncher was too terrified to notice. His nerves were in shreds. 'Tell it to stop,' he begged.

'LET'S TAKE A BREAK,' ordered the Prof.

Click. Whirr. The metal claw opened. Set Cruncher's hand free.

The Professor seemed hurt that Cruncher didn't like Claw as much as he did. He tried to reassure him.

'It's just a machine,' he told Cruncher. 'It only does what you tell it. It hasn't got a mind of its own.'

Suddenly, Claw rotated. Cruncher sprang back. One finger flipped up. It made a very rude gesture in the Prof's direction.

Cruncher goggled. 'Did you make it do that?' he asked Professor Kettles.

'Do what?' said the Prof. He wasn't even looking. He'd wandered away, was tapping computer keys.

Whirr. Click. The glittering silver claw retracted. The brutal hand curled up, like a huge, dead, silver spider.

'*Er*, nothing,' said Cruncher. He thought, *Was I seeing things?*

Professor Kettles flicked the power switch to OFF, shut down the whole crisp production line. The rumbling conveyor belt slowed. The fat stopped sizzling, started cooling down. Claw was as still and silent as the other machines. Switched off. Dead. All its strength and power gone.

Phew, thought Cruncher, relaxing.

He didn't like Claw at all. Even though it did make his favourite crisps.

'Take a look around,' the Prof invited him. 'I'm just checking our Spud Buddies chatroom. See if there's any hot news about potatoes. There might even be some young people, eager to become Spudlings.'

'*Spudlings?*' asked Cruncher.

'Yes, that's my fun name for our junior members – when we get some.'

'Don't hold your breath,' murmured Cruncher, as he skidded off to explore.

The old, wooden pulpit towered above him, as high as a watchtower. It must have fitted in once, when this was a church. But now, surrounded by all this shiny, hi-tech machinery, it looked really out of place. There was a savage-looking eagle carved at the front of it. It had a cruel beak and talons and sharp, all-seeing eyes. And spread wings, for the preacher to rest his Bible on.

What's this? thought Cruncher. He'd just noticed it, by his feet. It was a black marble slab set in the floor. It had writing carved on it. Cruncher crouched down.

'*In memory of the Reverend Silas Smite,*' he read. '*Rector of this church. Died September 1753.*'

There were more words underneath, all smeary with grease. Cruncher could only just read them.

'*He Smote the Evil Potato and All Those Sinners who Sup Upon It.*'

Eh? thought Cruncher, frowning. He stood up, his dwindling crisp supply crackling in his pants. 'Who was this Silas Smite guy? And what was his problem with potatoes?'

Professor Kettles seemed not to hear. Or if he did, he chose not to answer. Instead he called out, 'Your grandad would be interested in this.'

'In what?' Cruncher skidded back to the computer. On his way he gave Claw a suspicious glance. It was bunched up, into a silver fist. Did it really flip a finger at the Professor?

Couldn't have, thought Cruncher, remembering what the Prof had said. *It's just a machine. It hasn't got a mind of its own.*

Professor Kettles was excited. He peered keenly at the screen.

'That space junk heading this way,' he said. 'I think I know what it is.'

'*Wow,*' said Cruncher. He forgot about Claw – and Silas Smite. 'I've got to tell Grandad.' He'd been tracking that bit of junk

for weeks. It was coming in from outer space!

'The word on the Web is,' said the Prof, 'that it's a controlled environment growth chamber.'

'Pardon?' Cruncher had been prepared to be thrilled. But now he was just puzzled. Outer space was like that. You thought it would be dead exciting – aliens, star wars, inter-galactic battles, stuff like that. But, actually, it was quite boring.

'You know I told you about the first potato grown in space?' the Professor was saying. 'Whose picture we've put on our Spud Buddies web site? To make it more interesting for kids?'

'Yeah,' yawned Cruncher.

Privately, he thought that if the Prof wanted kids like him to log on, he should have photos of rude potatoes. A competition even: The Rudest Potato Ever. The one he'd seen at school would win that. He sniggered again, just remembering it.

'Well, here's the picture,' the Professor was droning on, 'coming up on the screen.'

A weedy-looking plant flashed up, with limp leaves and the root swollen into a tiny spud. Underneath the plant, it said:

ONE SMALL STEP FOR POTATOES, ONE GIANT LEAP FOR VEGETABLES! IMPRESSIVE OR WHAT, SPUDLINGS?

'Huh,' said Cruncher, unimpressed.

But there was one thing about the Space Potato that did interest him.

'Professor Kettles, did they have Scavenger Worms on that space shuttle? Was that potato grown in astronaut –'

But the Prof was already speeding ahead, anxious to tell Cruncher the great news.

'Well, after that first spud, they tried lots of experiments, to make the potatoes grow better. Each one had its own little growth chamber. Some were sent up in unmanned space shuttles, with a video link back to Earth. So scientists could check on how well they were growing.'

A little light came on in Cruncher's brain. 'So, that's what this space junk is that Grandad's tracking? A growth chamber? With a potato plant inside?'

'You've got it!' said the Prof. 'Isn't it amazing? An unmanned space shuttle broke up, scattering space junk all over the place.

And one of the Spud Buddies – he's a space fanatic too, like your grandad – he heard Space Control in Houston saying, "We have a problem! We've lost contact with our potato."'

'Huh,' said Cruncher again.

He'd been expecting the space junk to be something much more glamorous. Even an astronaut's glove would have been better.

But it was even more of a non-event. Because the Professor said, 'Of course, if it ever gets here without completely burning up, the growth chamber will just be a lump of mangled metal. And there's no chance of the potato plant inside it surviving. No chance at all.'

Cruncher's tour of Chapel Crisps seemed to be at an end. The Professor was glued to the Spud Buddies web site. Cruncher thought he'd been forgotten.

But then the Prof said, rather desperately, 'Would you like to become our first Spudling? You get a free book: *One Thousand Fascinating Facts About Potatoes*.'

'*Errrr*,' said Cruncher.

'You get a cool, free T-shirt too,' coaxed the Professor. 'With *I'm A Spudling* printed across the front. All your friends will want one.'

'Sorry, must dash!' yelled Cruncher, wildly. 'Tell Grandad about that space junk.'

He raced out of the factory.

Phew, he thought, *that was a lucky escape.*

He didn't want to disappoint Prof Kettles. Tell him that he, Cruncher, wasn't a budding potato boffin. That he found potatoes really boring – even spuds from outer space. Unless, of course, they were made into crisps.

Grandad's Little Kingdom wasn't far. Cruncher could see it from here. Moonlight lit up the road, made it nearly as bright as day.

'The Prof could have given me some free samples,' Cruncher muttered.

His own crisp supply was running danger-ously low. He took out a bag, popped it with his dagger thumb. Shook his head at the words 'handmade'. Those words had a whole new meaning now. Not made by a sweet, apple-cheeked old granny. But by a mailed fist that could do embroidery – or crush your bones.

But Claw was only one of his worries. He had plenty of other things on his mind.

Who was Silas Smite? Was the first spud in space grown in astronaut poo? And just what *was* the snag with Scavenger Worms?

Pondering these questions, while giving

his crisps a merciless munching, Cruncher plodded on down the road.

Then *WHOOSH*! Something shot by overhead. Cruncher felt heat: a white-hot flash blinded him. He ducked. But it was already gone.

'What was that?' He gazed after it.

The fireball curved over the council tip. *BOOM!* The explosion echoed among the dark garbage mountains. The dazzling white light disappeared.

It's landed, thought Cruncher. *Was it the space junk? Grandad'll be over the moon!*

Grandad had secretly been hoping for this for years. Even though he said it would never happen.

Another light shone out from the council tip. Cruncher didn't see it. He was too busy hurrying to find Grandad.

It was the Little Waif, still standing on her dark mountain top. As the space junk slammed into the landfill site, the glow around her had suddenly became fiercer, stronger.

Now she blazed out, like a star.

Chapter Six

After Cruncher left, Professor Kettles stayed hunched at his computer screen.

Strange things were happening around him. The metal fist was still clenched, motionless. But the bright neon strips over the crisp production line had flickered and gone dim. Moonbeams were slanting in through the red stained glass. They fell on Silas Smite's memorial stone set in the church floor, lit it up like a splash of fresh blood in the gloom. The words '*Evil Potato*' blazed out, as if they were written in letters of fire.

But the Prof didn't notice.

'This is very interesting,' he murmured, his eyes fixed on the screen.

He was reading about spuds in space. About recent experiments where they'd tinkered about with potato genes to produce a new, super plant – one that could fight off all bugs and blights. They'd used genes from a wild potato – the kind Native Americans used to dig up and eat. It had sticky leaves that could catch insects.

They'd even tried growing the super spud in soil from the planet Mars. Martian soil was red powdery stuff, full of strange volcanic materials.

'Intriguing,' murmured Professor Kettles.

Suddenly, he heard a noise, over by the pulpit. A strange metallic sound – *Shwack! Shwack!* – like knives being clashed together. The Prof's head shot up. Not again. It wasn't one of the machines. He knew every rattle of his crisp production line by heart – every *whirr* and *clank* that Claw made. Besides, Claw wasn't in action now. It couldn't even unclench its fist unless he told it to.

Professor Kettles got up from the computer, stared over to the pulpit. Why had the lights in here grown so dim?

Something was happening. Over by the pulpit, a swirl of blackness separated itself from the other shadows. It seemed to have an energy all its own. It was whirling up the pulpit steps like a mini tornado. *Shwack! Shwack!*

That metallic sound seemed to be coming from inside it. The Prof could see glittering, like lightning inside a storm cloud.

Professor Kettles stared at it. He'd heard noises, seen movements in the dark lately. But nothing like this.

BOOM! You could hear the space junk crashlanding, even inside Chapel Crisps. But the Prof didn't have any time to think, *What's that?* because the conveyor belt started rumbling.

I didn't switch on the power, thought the Professor, bewildered.

But you could feel power, coming from somewhere – an electric charge that seemed to make the air crackle. That fizzed through his body, made his fingertips tingle and his hair frizz out through the holes in his hairnet.

He rushed to a box on the wall. Switched off the electricity for the whole factory. That should have shut everything down. But the crisp-making machinery just kept going as if it had a life of its own.

'This shouldn't be happening,' he moaned, staring helplessly around him.

The smell of burning rubber, then black smoke, came from the conveyor belt as it

screeched along, sending potatoes bouncing towards Claw.

Suddenly, Claw's metal fingers jerked open. Sparks spat from its silver talons. Claw snatched the first potato. *Rrrip*: skinned it. *Whop, whop, whop*: sliced it. *Ssss!* Chucked it in bubbling fat.

'LET'S TAKE A BREAK!' yelled the Professor, frantically. What was going on? He hadn't even told Claw, 'LET'S MAKE CRISPS.'

But Claw wouldn't obey. It was out of control! Peeling potatoes down to pea size, hurling dud spuds in all directions. Splattering hot fat up the walls. Surely it couldn't go faster? It was already a silver blur.

'Ow!' said Professor Kettles as a flying spud bounced off his bonce. He took cover under the computer desk.

Peeking out, he gazed at the black whirl-wind in the pulpit. It was glowing, as if it had a red furnace inside. First an arm came out, waving a pair of cruel-looking iron shears.

Schwack, schwack, went the shears as the blades clashed together. *Schwack, schwack*.

Then came a voice, like thunder from a storm cloud.

'Stand up, all ye potato-loving sinners!' it boomed. 'So I may chop at thee with my mighty shears!'

At last, the speaker showed himself. He stepped out of the fiery blackness. Leaned over the edge of the pulpit, rested his shears on the eagle's outspread wings. His burning eyes searched the church.

The Prof took one look at those fanatical eyes, those grey flowing locks. That hooky nose, with wide flaring nostrils, that could sniff mashed potatoes a mile off. And, most of all, that battered straw hat.

'Silas Smite!' gasped Professor Kettles.

That hat was Silas Smite's trademark. In it, the preacher tramped the moors, seeking out potato lovers. A straw hat like that should have made him look friendly. But it only made him look even more sinister. Like a mad scarecrow come to life.

The Reverend Smite had been dead for 250 years. Yet something had plucked him through time. He could speak. He seemed like flesh and blood.

The Prof was the world's top potato scientist. He was also a keen potato historian. He knew about Silas Smite, the spud-hating preacher. How, back in the eighteenth century, he'd sought out and punished anyone who so much as tasted a potato. He never showed any pity. Even if it was their only food. Even if, without it, they and their children would starve.

'Rather starve,' Silas Smite would thunder, clacking his cruel shears, 'than eat of the Devil's root!'

Oh yes, Prof Kettles knew all about Silas Smite. That's why his brain was shrieking at him, 'Run!'

But it was too late. The Reverend Smite had spotted him.

Silas Smite's whole body quaked with fury. His eyes blazed from under his scarecrow hat.

'I SEE WHAT THOU ART!' the preacher roared. He pointed a quivering arm down from the pulpit. What had he seen?

The Prof glanced down, at the tiny blue and crimson potato flower in his buttonhole. 'Oh no!' he breathed. He'd forgotten all about it. But it marked him out as a potato fan right away.

'Sinful wretch,' screamed Silas Smite. 'Come hither! That I may chop at thee!' He picked up his shears from the eagle's wings.

But something gave Professor Kettles strength. All of a sudden, he was racing across the greasy floor to the exit, crashing the big wooden church doors shut behind him.

Outside, the Prof collapsed against the church wall. He slumped there, panting, his brain trying to cope with what he'd just seen.

He peeped back through a stained-glass window. It was mayhem in there. His entire factory had gone berserk! Some kind of mysterious force had taken it over. Lights were flashing madly, machinery was running at top speed. Claw was making crisps like a maniac, peeling, slicing, frying. Could the extendable arm stand the strain?

Up in the pulpit, Silas Smite was still screeching. His thin, skull-like face was twisted with hatred. The Prof couldn't hear the words. But he could guess it was something very insulting about potatoes.

'What's happening?' groaned Professor Kettles, his head in his hands.

His little potato boffin's world was falling apart.

'Potatoes are the Devil's root,' chanted a zombie-like voice, right in his ear.

The Prof whirled round: 'Who said that?'

There was no one behind him.

It was you, he thought, shocked. *You said it.* But how could that be? In his whole life, a bad word about potatoes had never passed his lips. He was their greatest admirer, their most loyal fan.

Then he realized. Almost without knowing it, he'd been looking deep into Silas Smite's eyes. They burned with potato-hating zeal. They stared into your very soul. Brainwashed you to think like him.

You're doing it again, Professor Kettles warned himself.

He was staring, through the window, into those scorching eyes, like a rabbit hypnotized by car headlights. But he just couldn't tear his gaze away.

'Potatoes are the Devil's –' he heard himself saying.

'No!' the Professor screamed at himself. He slapped a hand over his eyes, so he couldn't see Silas Smite any more.

'I will never betray potatoes. *Never*,' he whispered to himself, clenching his fists, until the knuckles were white as bone.

But his voice, meant to be firm and defiant, sounded shaky. The Prof knew he still wasn't safe. Anyone without his strong loyalty to spuds could easily have their mind invaded. Be persuaded that potatoes were the most wicked things on the planet and should be wiped off the face of the Earth.

The Professor shuddered. A world without spuds just didn't bear thinking about.

He started running again, on wobbly legs.

Inside the factory, while the Prof escaped and the mad preacher roared from the pulpit, 'Repent, potato lovers. Hellfire awaits thee!', something drastic was happening to Claw.

Claw was rotating at high speed. Its metal skin was hot and smoking. Its silver talons shot out to grab another spud. They never made it. There was a terrible wrenching sound as Claw's wrist joint gave way. Snapped clean in two. Claw crashed to the floor.

It lay there helpless, like a giant silver crab on its back. Its fingers twitched madly, still trying to peel, slice and fry, then folded up, into a fist.

A puddle of crisp fat spread around it on the floor. Claw looked clapped out, finished.

But inside that metal skin, it was still functioning. It shouldn't have been. But, ever since the space junk started heading this way, strange power surges had done weird things to Claw's robot brain. It had begun having thoughts, even feelings of its own, during the long, lonely nights of crisp making. And its main feeling was, *I want to be free.*

Now it had what it wanted. It was free from slavery. From human voice commands. From making crisps 24/7, with no holidays, not even Christmas.

The smallest silver talon uncurled.

Free!

Cautiously, it stretched out all its talons, feeling around. It didn't have eyes. But, like the antennae of an insect, the sensors in its fingertips gave it all the information it needed.

What would be its next move? Now it had the whole wide world to explore? Now it could make its own choices?

It should have been jumping for joy, doing backwards flips. Instead, it snatched back its talons, curled up into a ball.

Suddenly, Claw felt very lost and alone. It almost wished the Professor was here to give it orders. It wished it hadn't flipped fingers, or chucked spuds at him.

Its circuits were overloading with all this

stress. It just couldn't cope. For the first time ever, the metal gauntlet felt fear.

It scuttled under the conveyor belt, to hide.

'Grandad!' shouted Cruncher. 'You in there?'

He'd already checked the little shed, the one where Grandad tracked space junk. Green blips were still pinging across the screen. But there was no one to watch them. The shed was empty. And Grandad's chair was tipped over, as if he'd left in a hurry.

Now Cruncher was rattling the door of Grandad's big shed. The one he always kept locked.

'You in there, Grandad?' he called again. 'About that space junk – guess what? I know what it is!'

There were curtains over the shed windows so you couldn't see in. What was Grandad hiding in there? Cruncher found a crack in the shed wall, jammed his eye to it. Grandad had left a light on. But it was still very dim. Cruncher could see some kind of large vehicle in the gloom.

It's a bin van! he thought. Just like the ones that rumbled in and out of the landfill site, all day long.

It had ENVIRONMENTAL SERVICES written on the side in big green letters, just like all the others. But, wait a minute, there were extra words. Someone had painted OUT OF THIS WORLD in front of ENVIRON-MENTAL SERVICES. And underneath it said, WE CLEAN UP – IN SPACE.

Cruncher sighed, 'For heaven's sake.'

He knew Grandad was always banging on about how there was big money in clean-ing up space junk. But Cruncher never dreamed it had gone this far. Grandad had got himself a vehicle. Even a name for his company.

'Out Of This World Environmental Services,' murmured Cruncher. Not bad.

But what about the adjustments to the bin van? All the stuff you'd need for going into space, catching high-speed junk? Cruncher stared hard. He couldn't see anything different.

It's just an ordinary bin van, thought Cruncher scornfully – cab at the front, crusher at the back. It wasn't even the latest model. Just some battered old bin van that should have been on the scrap heap long ago.

'Huh,' said Cruncher. And he'd almost

been tempted to take Out Of This World Environmental Services seriously.

He was worried about Grandad. Sometimes Cruncher thought he lived in fantasy land.

But where *was* Grandad anyhow? Cruncher couldn't get into the caravan. It was locked. But he could see through the windows that Grandad wasn't inside.

Cruncher shrugged. *He's probably out there, searching for that space junk.* He couldn't get too excited about it himself, now he knew what it was.

'Might as well go home,' he suddenly decided.

He'd been planning to stay the night. But who knows how long Grandad would be? And he didn't want to hang around here on his own. There was something scary about this place tonight. He could feel it in his bones – a sort of spooky electric tingling. Sense it in the air – a growing menace, as if there were dark forces gathering, somewhere very close. He'd felt it on the council tip when he and the Prof were dumping potato sludge. But now it was here too. And it was a thousand times more powerful.

Cruncher shuddered.

He was halfway home, when he heard loud laughter from across the street.

'Hey, look at that prat! He's wearing a pink hairnet!'

'*Aaaaargh!*' Cruncher snatched it off, stamped it into the gutter. He rushed away, his trousers crackling loudly.

He could hear the hoots of laughter right down the road.

He was glad he'd sharpened that thumb-nail. Otherwise that right-hand thumb might have slid into his mouth, just for comfort. Think of the shame! Caught wearing a pink hairnet and thumbsucking. He'd never be able to hold his head up in this town again.

He yanked a bag of Chapel Crisps from his knee pocket. Attacked it wildly. *Slash*. His dagger thumb ripped it open. *KERRUNCH*. Take that, crisps. Total demolition!

He blew up the bag and burst it. *BLAM*.

'Cave*man*.'

He strode home, feeling like he could take on a sabre-toothed tiger and a woolly mammoth, both at the same time.

'I'll give up crisps tomorrow,' he promised himself.

*

The potato had finished its long journey, through the dark, silent vastness of space. Snug in its growth chamber, it hadn't died, as Professor Kettles had predicted. The chamber had kept it alive with water, light and food. Even when these ran out, it had carried on growing. The Martian soil gave it all the nutrients it needed.

Science had never seen anything like this plant. It had been genetically engineered anyway. And other, even stranger things, happen to a super spud growing in outer space in alien soil.

Cramped in its shoebox-sized growth chamber, the potato plant hadn't been able to grow much. But it was making up for that.

When the growth chamber crashlanded, it had split open. It was a mangled wreck now. But that didn't matter. The space spud didn't need it any more. The impact had thrown the spud clear and buried it deep in a garbage mountain, which acted like a giant compost heap. The spud instantly began growing at top speed. Its roots, even in the space of a few hours, spread quickly underground. There were nasty things lurking under the rotting rubbish. Toxic chemicals, pockets of highly

explosive methane gas. But none of these things stopped the Space Potato. In fact, it seemed to thrive on them.

Bushy stems appeared on the surface. As they waved in the night air, they seemed to feed on the energy forces that had gathered here. As though this insignificant spot, with the crisp factory, Grandad's Little Kingdom and the council tip, had become the most important place on the planet.

As the night passed, the potato plant grew bigger, stronger.

Even Prof Kettles, who was a potato fan, thought it was OK to make them into crisps. But this was a potato that couldn't be sliced up, mashed or made into waffles.

This was a potato with attitude.

Chapter Seven

Cruncher woke up yelling, 'No!'

He'd dreamed that there was a world shortage of Chapel Crisps. That it was on the news: 'Crisp fans are rioting in the streets. Cheese-and-onion are changing hands for one thousand pounds a bag.'

'Stay calm,' the newsreader advised the public. 'There's no need to panic buy.'

Better stock up, thought Cruncher, throwing off his duvet. He'd only got one packet left. He'd scoffed the others as a midnight snack. He shook his hair. Crisp crumbs flew out like dandruff. He had a quick scratch down his pyjama bottoms. Those crisp crumbs got everywhere.

He calmed himself down, 'No need to rush. It was just a nightmare.' There'd be plenty of Chapel Crisps in the shops.

But he leapt up anyway. He had things to do. He had to go to Grandad's Little Kingdom. Tell him the news – that the space junk was just a growth chamber, and that the Space Potato inside it was a puny-looking, unimpressive plant. And that it couldn't have survived anyway.

Like him, Grandad might feel a bit let down. Grandad was a strange bloke. When he talked about waste disposal, he was very down-to-earth. Discussing astronaut poo or Scavenger Worms didn't bother him.

By the way, Cruncher made a mental note, *I must ask him what the snag is, with Scavenger Worms.*

But, at the same time, Grandad was a guy with vision. He was a dreamer, a stargazer.

He'd longed all his life for space junk to land on his doorstep. *What a shame*, thought Cruncher, *that when it finally did, it was something so boring.*

Cruncher sighed. Life was like that. Full of disappointments. Like his self-improvement kick. He was getting nowhere with his crisp problem. He was probably even more crazy about them now, since he'd discovered that caveman feeling.

But *Hey!* thought Cruncher. *Every cloud had a silver lining*. He hadn't sucked his thumb last night. In spite of that shocking dream about a Chapel Crisp shortage.

Cruncher felt himself getting scared and sweaty just remembering it.

Get a grip, he told himself. *Just call at the corner shop. Get more supplies.*

On the way to the shop, he took out his dagger thumb and admired it. Men grew their fingernails really long in Ancient China. Cruncher had been to a museum once and seen a little silver sheath that you slipped on your finger end. FOR PROTECTING LONG FINGERNAILS, the sign beside it had said.

I need something like that, he thought.

It would be tragic if that dagger thumbnail got broken now. Just when it was working so brilliantly.

Cheered up that at least he'd cracked one of his bad habits, Cruncher bounced confidently into the corner shop: 'Ten packets of Chapel Crisps, please.'

'We haven't got any,' said the shop assistant before he could even tell her what flavours.

'*Aaaaaargh!*' Cruncher's brain went spinning into chaos. His whole world collapsed.

He stared at the shop assistant. 'Pardon?' he said shakily. A little gleam of hope still flickered. Nightmares never come true, everyone knows that. Maybe he just hadn't heard right. Maybe his ears were playing cruel tricks.

But she repeated those awful words: 'We haven't got any. The guy who owns the factory –'

'Professor Kettles,' Cruncher chipped in.

'Yeah, well he was supposed to make an early morning delivery. But he never showed up.'

Cruncher staggered out of the shop, his brain still struggling to cope with the shocking news.

Don't panic. Don't panic, he told himself, as he struggled to stay calm.

But he only had *one* packet left! He patted his trouser pocket, to make sure it was safe. He thought wildly, *Where else can I buy them?* But he knew from experience, that wherever else Prof Kettles sold them, it wasn't round here.

It was all the more reason to go hurrying

towards Grandad's Little Kingdom and Chapel Crisps.

He's gonna have *to give me some free samples now*, thought Cruncher.

At every step he was reminded that his crisp supplies were at rock bottom. Instead of a loud, reassuring crackle coming from his trousers, there was just the tiniest rustle. It was such a sad, melancholy sound, like dead leaves whispering in the wind.

Cruncher reached the edge of town. There was the council tip, spread out below him. But what was going on? There was no snarl of bin vans, clank of JCBs. Cruncher had expected that. It was Saturday – the tip was shut. Only Grandad's Little Kingdom stayed open seven days a week. What he hadn't expected was the low, black clouds that hung over the tip, Chapel Crisps and Grandad's Little Kingdom. There was clear blue sky everywhere else. But on that one spot, there seemed to be a storm brewing.

Sssss! An electric flash hissed from clouds to garbage mountains. For one second the tip was lit by an eerie blue glow. Then got swallowed again by darkness.

Lightning! thought Cruncher.

That TV weathergirl had really got it wrong this morning. Her map had been crowded with smiley suns.

Cruncher hurried down to the tip. At the high wire fence that surrounded it, he was suddenly plunged from sunlight into shadow. As if he was crossing a border. From a bright, cheerful country to one that was wild, dark and sinister.

Outside Grandad's Little Kingdom there was a yellow, three-wheeled car waiting. It had its headlights switched on. And a pair of enormous moose antlers strapped to its roof.

The driver wound down his window. 'Strange weather,' he said to Cruncher. 'It's sunny back in town.' He jabbed at his watch. 'Shouldn't he have opened up by now?'

'*Er*, yeah,' nodded Cruncher. It was really unlike Grandad to be late opening up. He ran this place like clockwork. Surely he wasn't still out looking for space junk?

But the gate was padlocked. The CLOSED sign was still up.

Cruncher shouted, 'Grandad!' There was no answer. Where was he? He should be making breakfast. You should be able to smell bacon frying.

On Saturdays, he always made an extra bacon sarnie for Cruncher.

Cruncher peered anxiously through the wire. It looked as gloomy as a graveyard in there. There were no signs of life at all. He tried to shake it off, that feeling of dread. It was gripping his mind again. Like last night, only stronger.

'Grandad?' He rattled the gate. 'Where are you?' He hated how feeble and scared his voice sounded.

'Better take these home then,' said the driver, pointing up to the roof-rack. 'I'll dump them some other time.'

Cruncher almost said, 'I'll have 'em.' They'd look good on his bedroom wall.

But the little yellow car was already trundling away, so top-heavy with moose antlers it seemed it might topple over at any moment. But still the driver tried to make it go faster.

And Cruncher knew the driver had felt it too. That sense of something menacing, waiting to spring. As if this spot on the planet had been taken over by malevolent powers – for their own evil purposes.

Cruncher mocked himself, *You've been watching too many horror movies.*

But when he shouted 'Grandad!' again, his voice sounded even more lost and afraid.

Time for that caveman feeling, thought Cruncher. It was his last packet. But he didn't feel too desperate. He could get fresh supplies from Chapel Crisps. It was only five minutes' walk away.

I'll go round there straightaway, he decided.

'But what if Professor Kettles is missing too?' a tiny, scared voice in his head suggested. After all, he hadn't done his crisp deliveries this morning.

Rrrip. Cruncher attacked the crisp bag with his dagger thumb. He already felt bolder. *KERRUNCH.* He was giving his first crisps a good mashing when he suddenly stopped, in mid-crunch. The back of his neck was prickling. Someone was watching him. He was sure of it.

'Grandad?' He spun round.

She was behind the fence of the landfill site. She looked like the pictures of poor beggar children Cruncher had seen in his school history book. Her tatty dress looked rough and scratchy, as if it was made from an old coal sack.

He stared, a mess of soggy crisp wobbling on his tongue. So Grandad hadn't been seeing things – his ragged little girl *did* exist.

The Little Waif stared back at Cruncher with huge, solemn eyes. She seemed solid, real. But at the same time, there was an unearthly glow around her that made her look like a ghost – or an angel.

Cruncher's shocked gaze took in her white, pinched face, her smoke-blackened dress, her bare feet, frosty-blue with cold.

She stretched a skinny arm through the fence. 'Hungry, Master,' she said, pitifully.

Cruncher sprang forwards: *What's she on about?* he thought, bewildered. *I'm not her master.* But her other word, 'hungry', couldn't be misunderstood.

Half horrified, half embarrassed, he thrust his last packet of crisps into her hand. 'Here, have these. I don't want 'em.'

As her twig-like fingers clutched the bag, Cruncher had another shock. He could feel his heart give a great, sickening jolt. On her right hand, she had a long, sharpened thumbnail, just like his.

Was she a thumbsucker too?

She was staring, bewildered, at the crisps he'd just given her. As if she didn't know what to do with them.

Where'd she come from? thought Cruncher. It looked like she'd never seen a crisp packet before.

'They're made of *potatoes*,' said Cruncher, nodding encouragement. 'Try one. They taste good.'

He might just as well have said, 'They're deadly poison.' Because the Little Waif dropped the bag on the ground and backed away from it.

'*Taters?*' she stammered, her eyes wild and terrified.

She looked longingly at the bag. Some crisps had spilled out on to the mud. She reached out. Then snatched her hand back, as if the crisps had turned into hissing snakes.

'No, I durstn't! I durstn't eat taters!'

And she whisked away. The clouds cast their murky shadows over the council tip. But Cruncher could still see her as she scrambled up a garbage mountain, because she shone out among the stinking rubbish piles, with such a pure, white radiance.

Cruncher felt rocked to the core. What had

he just seen? A real kid? A ghost? An angel? He was still too stunned to try and work it out.

Then he heard the padlock chain clattering behind him.

'Grandad? Where've you been?' demanded Cruncher.

But it wasn't Grandad. It was Professor Kettles, looking out from Grandad's Little Kingdom. What was he doing in there?

'Let me in,' said Cruncher.

The Prof opened the padlock with Grandad's spare set of keys.

He looked a wreck. His white coat was crumpled. The potato flower in his buttonhole had gone limp. Didn't he know he still had his pink hairnet on?

Words were tumbling out of his mouth. What was he drivelling on about? Cruncher didn't care. The Prof wasn't the only one who was cracking up.

'I've seen her,' Cruncher cried, pointing into the council tip. 'She's up there. That light that shines like a star!'

Professor Kettles didn't even look. He grabbed Cruncher by the arm. 'Ow,' said Cruncher. 'Leggo.'

The Prof's frenzied fingers only gripped

tighter. Eyes that seemed half crazy stared into Cruncher's own.

'I've seen HIM,' raved Professor Kettles. 'Silas Smite. The potato-hating preacher. I've seen him, large as life!'

Halfway up a garbage mountain, behind a stack of old mattresses, the Space Potato was as high as a pine tree and still growing.

It had dark-green leaves like tongues, each one furry with sticky hairs. Its stems waved in the air as if it was sniffing for something. Things were happening under the ground too. Roots, like white wriggling worms, sprouted from the Space Potato. Some were thick as your arm. They pushed their way through the putrid garbage. Every so often, the root swelled into another potato. Soon, those potatoes, too, would send up stems and sticky leaves into the murky daylight. Soon there would be a whole army of Space Potato plants on the council tip.

But, for the moment, there was just one. The mother plant. The one that gave birth to all the others.

A seagull came flapping this way. The plant stems stopped waving. Curled up like ferns, became sneakily still – as if they were waiting. The seagull was right overhead. Suddenly, a stem whiplashed out, wrapping itself round the seagull, the sticky leaves holding it fast.

With one surprised squawk, the seagull was dragged down into the writhing plant.

This wasn't just a plant that defended itself against danger, like its wild potato ancestor. This was a potato that hunted for prey – a predator potato that attacked first.

Chapter Eight

Professor Kettles had calmed down a bit. He was drinking tea from a Golden Jubilee teacup (the one Grandad had salvaged from a skip and glued back together). But the Professor's cup still rattled <u>against the</u> saucer.

'It was a terrible shock,' he told Cruncher.

They were sitting in Grandad's little shed, with the radar screen bleeping away behind them.

'I've been here all night,' said Professor Kettles. 'I barricaded the door with deck-chairs. Then I heard you yelling "Grandad!"' The Prof's cup clattered uncontrollably.

'No way am I going back to Chapel Crisps,' said the Professor, shuddering. 'Not while that maniac's about. Wild horses wouldn't drag me.'

He didn't mention the brainwashing. How, for a brief moment, Silas Smite had made him hate potatoes. It had been the most shameful few seconds of his life.

'This Smite guy. Is he a *ghost*?' asked Cruncher, feeling a chill chase down his spine as he said the word.

The Professor shook his head. 'I'm not sure. He seems more real than that. He's solid, he can speak. It's as if he's alive. But just in the wrong time zone.'

'That's like the kid I saw,' Cruncher butted in. 'This ragged kid on the tip. Grandad's seen her. He calls her the Little Waif. She looks real. But I thought, "Is she an angel?" Cos she shines all silvery, like the moon.'

'I've seen her too,' said Professor Kettles.

'You think *she*'s from the past?' asked Cruncher. 'Like that Silas Smite guy?'

'I don't know,' said the Professor. 'But rather strange things are happening here.'

'*Rather strange* things?' echoed Cruncher. He could think of much better descriptions. Like *buttock-clenchingly*, *toe-curlingly petrifying* things, for instance.

'Things that break all scientific laws,' the Professor continued, as if in a daze. 'It's ever

since that space junk started heading this way . . .'

'I think it's landed,' Cruncher butted in again. 'Last night. I saw this fireball. Heard this big *BOOM*! I think it's out there somewhere, on the council tip.'

'So *that's* what it was.'

The Professor's face grew deathly pale. He remembered the *BOOM* last night, just as the machines started up and Silas Smite appeared. A muscle twitched in his cheek like a tiny heartbeat. It couldn't be a coincidence, could it? Silas Smite and the space junk, bursting on to the scene at precisely the same moment. Even if one had travelled through space to get here and the other through time?

'When great powers clash,' the Professor murmured, 'you get critical mass. Rules of space and time get broken. Massive energy is released –'

'Pardon?' said Cruncher.

'And anything near gets caught in the shock waves,' said the Professor. 'And crushed.'

'What are you on about?' cried Cruncher. 'What great powers?'

'Expect *anything*,' said the Professor, darkly. 'It's chaos out there.'

'What about Grandad? I can't find him.'

But the Professor wasn't listening. His eyes looked haunted and far away. As if he was lost in some private nightmare.

Cruncher had a sudden brainwave. 'Stupid, why didn't you check the caravan?' he scolded himself. Grandad had probably just overslept. 'He's probably still in bed, snoring.'

Prof Kettles was mumbling something. 'The machines are running on their own. Claw's out of control, slicing, frying –'

Suddenly, his teacup clattered like castanets. Another dreadful vision had invaded his mind. 'His eyes,' he moaned, trembling, 'whatever you do, don't look into his eyes.'

But Cruncher didn't hear any of it. He was already gone, rushing out to the caravan. Past the shed, where Grandad kept his big secret – the old bin van that was supposed to clean up space junk.

Out Of This World Environmental Services, thought Cruncher, shaking his head as he dashed by. He didn't know whether to laugh or cry.

He thumped on Grandad's caravan. 'Wake up, Grandad. I want my bacon sarnie.'

Then he saw there was a note stuck to

the door: 'Gone out. Still searching for space junk.' That hadn't been there last night.

Cruncher tried the door. It was locked. He peered through the windows.

Grandad's bed was rumpled. He must have come back, snatched some sleep and gone out early to start searching again.

He stared at the forbidding garbage mountains, with spooky blue flashes of lightning crackling round the tops. Grandad was out there, somewhere.

I've got to find him, thought Cruncher. *Warn him about what the Prof said: Great powers clashing, critical mass, shock waves.*

He wasn't sure what it meant but it sounded dangerous. He didn't want Grandad caught in the middle of it. Or that Little Waif. She needed help too. She needed a good feed, one of Grandad's big breakfasts. Her fingers were as thin as umbrella spokes.

That reminded Cruncher: *She had a dagger thumb.*

She was such a strange, glowing creature. Half human, half supernatural. Where she came from, who she was, was a mystery. But Cruncher wasn't scared of her. He felt they shared something. That long thumbnail was a sign. They were both members of the Secret Society of Thumbsuckers.

'Ex-thumbsuckers,' Cruncher corrected himself.

She'd probably busted the habit now, just like he had. But, like him, she still kept her nail pointed. Just in case, in stressful situations, she ever felt that thumb sliding towards her mouth again.

Cruncher felt he already knew lots about her. But there were still big questions to ask. Where were her mum and dad? They must be really cruel parents, abandoning her on a rubbish dump. And why was she so scared of potatoes? People had phobias about loads of things: spiders, sharks, snakes. But he'd never, ever, met anyone who was petrified of spuds.

'Right,' Cruncher told himself. 'I'm going in now.' He walked slowly out of Grandad's Little Kingdom, over to the great metal gates of the council tip. He'd already thought, *Bet they're locked.* He'd have to go and get Grandad's spare keys from Professor Kettles.

But when he touched them, the gates clanged wide open, as if inviting him in. Cruncher sprang back, startled. Grandad

91

must have been so excited by the space junk, he'd forgotten to lock them behind him.

Cruncher stared through. He was on a rescue mission. But those garbage mountains looked so dark and grim. Like the landscape of nightmares, where all sorts of monsters lurked, just waiting to leap out at you. And what about those potato sludge lagoons? They could suck you under like quicksand. Professor Kettles had said so.

Suddenly Cruncher had a desperate longing. He needed some crisp therapy, to give his courage an extra boost.

But then he remembered. *Dumbo. What did you do that for?*

He'd given his last packet of crisps to the Little Waif. And did she appreciate his great sacrifice? No, she'd hurled his gift to the ground.

Cruncher thought, *Maybe I could still eat 'em.*

He could see them through the wire, where they'd spilled out of the bag. But they were sticky with the slimy green ooze that came seeping up from the rotting rubbish. Even a crisp fanatic like Cruncher couldn't face them. Besides, they were all soggy now. Their crackle quotient would be zero. And without that crackle, you just couldn't get that cave-man feeling.

Cruncher searched in all his trouser pockets. Maybe he'd missed a bag.

Fat chance, he thought. He already knew it was hopeless. He might be shambolic about all sorts of things. But when it came to his crisp supply, he was super-efficient. He *always* knew how many bags he had left, what flavour they were, what pocket they were in.

Cruncher frowned. There was a struggle going on inside him. He wanted to be a hero. Step through those Gates of Doom.

Yesterday, that name had seemed over the top. But not now. Even standing out here he could feel it – that vengeful power. As if the council tip was a great witch's cauldron in which evil spells were being brewed. He needed some back-up.

The Professor was no good. 'He's just gone to pieces,' sighed Cruncher, shaking his head. There was only one thing he could rely on.

'Crisps,' he told himself. And they had to be Chapel Crisps. Preferably cheese-and-onion.

He started hurrying along the road to the crisp factory.

'Nip in,' Cruncher told himself. 'Grab some. Nip out.'

But what about this Silas Smite character? Had Professor Kettles really seen him? Cruncher didn't believe it. Not that Silas Smite had somehow materialized. But that he'd ever existed in the first place. A potato-hating preacher – who thought spuds were sinful? Cruncher shook his head. How could you take a guy like that *seriously*?

He pushed at the church door. It creaked open. He slipped inside.

Back in Grandad's little shed, Professor Kettles was staring at the radar screen. Little green blips whizzed all over it. But he didn't see them. He was thinking about Silas Smite and Robin's Corner, the burned-out village buried under the garbage mountains.

Back in the eighteenth century, Robin's Corner had been Silas Smite's favourite hunting ground. He was a holy terror. Peasants quaked in their hovels when he was on the prowl. His great flaring nostrils could detect boiling spuds from miles away. He'd stand outside the church and sniff the wind: 'I smell potatoes!'

Then he'd track that smell down. Kick over your cooking pot and stamp your dinner into the dirt.

And even if you weren't cooking potatoes, he could still get you. He would burst in, eyes blazing, shears clashing – 'Show me thy thumbs.'

The peasants of Robin's Corner were poor. Often, in winter, potatoes were their only food. And they couldn't afford cutlery. So they kept their right-hand thumbnails long, to scrape the skins off their spuds. 'Potato thumbs' they were called in those days.

And if Silas Smite spotted a potato thumb, he would roar at the quivering wretch before him: 'You shameless sinner. You have supped on the Devil's root! Come hither. Vengeance is mine, saith the Lord!'

And it was no good running. He'd pursue you over miles of moorland, his great shears snapping, his battered straw hat glinting in the sun. He'd never give up. His hatred of potatoes drove him on. Those thin, black-trousered legs would never tire. And then, when he caught you . . .

Professor Kettles gave a great shudder. It was the jolt he needed. It shook him out of his trance.

Are you just going to sit here? he fumed at himself. *Let that crazy potato-hating fanatic wreck your factory? Run your machines into the ground?*

It was Claw he was most concerned about. Without Claw, he could never achieve his ambition of making the perfect crisp.

Heaven knows how those energy surges have messed up its circuits, he thought. *I might have to program it all over again.*

But he could feel his heart fluttering. The preacher was a powerful enemy. He could mess up your mind.

Professor Kettles put up a hand to scratch his head. Why did it feel so itchy? Of course, he still had his hairnet on. He tugged it off. A shower of crisps came with it.

Some landed in his lap. He absent-mindedly munched one.

It shattered to bits in his mouth. *Kerrunch.*

'Caveman,' murmured the Professor, half embarrassed.

He stuffed in a whole handful. *KER-RUNCH.* The explosion rattled around in his skull. *KERRUNCH!* His molars worked fiercely. He gave them a savage mangling. Those crisps didn't stand a chance. They were mush.

'*Caveman!*' said the Professor again – this time, with feeling.

Cruncher was right. Eating Chapel Crisps did make you feel like a champion. He felt ready to face anything now. Even Silas Smite. He sprang out of the deckchair before the effects wore off.

He strode boldly to the door.

He was going to reclaim his factory from that spud-hating menace. And rescue Claw, the ultimate crisp-making machine.

Chapter Nine

Cruncher stood just inside the church door. It was dark and silent. He could hear his own heart beating. To him, it seemed as loud as bongo drums.

The crisp production line was in gloom. The machines were still. A smell of burning rubber and hot fat hung in the air.

Where was Claw? Cruncher couldn't see the metal fist. But Claw wasn't what he was looking for.

'Crisps, crisps, where are you?' wondered Cruncher. He felt an urgent need for one of those wild, caveman moments.

He found three lonely crisps on the cooling tray. *Kerrunch*. That salty taste exploded on his tongue.

'Cheese-and-onion!' His favourite. He felt better already.

Under the conveyor belt, Claw's sharp, silver talons quivered. They picked up the vibration of Cruncher's footsteps.

Cruncher saw a door that said STORE-ROOM. He skated towards it over the greasy floor. 'Bet they keep whole boxes of crisps in there.'

There was no sign of a spud-smiting preacher.

What did he smite 'em with, a spud masher? thought Cruncher, chuckling at his little joke.

Shwack, schwack.

What's that noise? thought Cruncher, peering through the gloom.

'SINNER!' A thunderous cry echoed through the church. Cruncher nearly jumped out of his skin.

First a battered straw hat, then two eyes, blazing with hatred, rose above the pulpit.

'It's *him*.' Cruncher felt a deathly chill inside, as if his heart had turned to ice. His whole body was one big shiver.

'THOU SINNER!' roared the Reverend, pointing a quivering arm down at Cruncher. 'Thou hast a potato thumb!'

What? Cruncher's panicking brain screamed at him. *What's he on about?* But then

Silas Smite's other arm appeared. It was waving a pair of glinting shears.

Schwack, schwack. He clashed the blades together. 'Vengeance is mine, saith the Lord! Come hither, sinner. I want thy thumb!'

Schwack, schwack.

This time, the mad preacher's meaning seemed crystal clear. Cruncher's brain shrieked at him, *Run!*

He took off. But his feet slipped from under him. He crashed full length on to the stone floor, beside the conveyor belt.

For a second, he was stunned. Then he felt something brushing his right hand, light as snowflakes. That creepy tickling felt familiar. *It couldn't be.*

Hardly daring to breathe, he turned his head. He saw something brutal, medieval, glinting under the conveyor belt.

'Claw!'

How did the metal gauntlet get free? It looked really gruesome, like something out of a horror film. Red wires were trailing from its severed wrist. Its talons had closed like a silver cage around Cruncher's dagger thumb. He was trapped.

But someone else wanted Cruncher's

thumb. Silas Smite was roaring, 'Do not seek to hide, sinner. Thy thumb must be forfeit. Come forth and take thy punishment.'

'Let me go,' Cruncher ordered Claw, in a panic. Claw couldn't hear, like humans do. Instead, it picked up speech vibrations. But its robot brain was only programmed to recognize certain words. What Cruncher was saying just didn't compute.

Then Cruncher remembered the correct commands.

'LET'S TAKE A BREAK,' he whispered, as loud as he dared.

Nothing happened. Why didn't Claw's metal fingers click open?

'Oh no,' groaned Cruncher, 'I forgot to be American.' He tried again, 'LET'S TAKE A BREAK.'

Still Claw didn't obey. 'It's my American accent, it's rubbish,' groaned Cruncher.

'*Where art thou, potato lover?*'

Suddenly, amazingly, Claw's talons clicked open. They'd finished scanning.

I'm free, thought Cruncher.

Cruncher snatched his hand back, staggered off into the shadows.

He didn't know Claw's robot brain had

identified him: *There was that other claw again!* The armoured hand had no idea it scared the pants off people. Inside, it felt like an orphan child. It needed love and protection and a place to belong. It went scuttling after Cruncher, its fingertips sensing his every move.

If it had been human, it might have shouted, 'Wait for me, Mummy!'

Silas Smite, full of righteous fury, was also chasing Cruncher through the church. But for very different reasons.

Schwack. Schwack.

The preacher was more powerful now, much more powerful than he had been back in the eighteenth century. For the past few weeks, he'd been an unseen menace, an invisible presence, prowling around Chapel Crisps. But gradually, he'd got stronger, more solid. Until, just last night, he'd suddenly burst through the time barrier, like a man-eating shark leaping up from the deep. With his potato hatred burning fiercer than ever.

The world had ignored his warnings. And now it was in deadly peril – from a potato more evil than even he had ever imagined.

'Beware potatoes!' said Silas Smite, as he

cornered Cruncher by the storeroom. 'Do not trust them. They are the enemy. They are the instrument of the Devil! They are plotting the ruin of mankind. That was what I preached. In sermons three hours long. But did anyone listen?'

Cruncher didn't answer. He was too busy watching those shears, as Silas Smite swiped them this way, that. Their glitter left a trail in the air like a sparkler.

Cruncher hid his dagger thumb behind his back.

Silas Smite answered his own question: 'No,' he raved, his eyes wild and fiery under his battered straw hat. 'No one listened. They would not repent of their sinful, potato-loving ways.'

He rattled his shears, waved them in the air like a sabre. 'And now they are in peril. From the most fiendish potato of them all. But It and I shall do battle. It is our destiny. The power of potatoes shall not prevail.'

Cruncher's brain shrieked at him, *He's totally off his rocker!*

He tried to dodge under those snapping blades. But there was no escape.

'Show me thy potato thumb,' commanded

Silas Smite, clashing his cruel shears.

'No!' shrieked Cruncher, white with terror. 'What you gonna do?' he cried, even though he had a pretty good idea.

Unseen by both of them, Claw was creeping up closer to Cruncher, like an armoured spider.

'No!' cried Cruncher again. Instinctively, he raised his right hand to shield himself.

Big mistake.

The shears came slicing down: *Schwack*.

'Another trophy for my hatband,' said Silas Smite, picking something off the floor.

Cruncher stared down at his thumb. It was still there! His knees buckled – he felt sick and dizzy. He stared up at Silas Smite's scarecrow hat. And saw, for the first time, that tucked into his hatband were long thumbnails, rows of them. Babies' thumbnails, pink and fragile as seashells. Yellow, horny thumbnails from ancient peasants. And among them now, was Cruncher's anti-thumbsucking device. That long, sharp talon he'd been so proud of.

But he never even thought about that. He was so relieved that the preacher hadn't lopped off his whole thumb.

'You scumbag! You nearly gave me a heart

attack!' That's what Cruncher started to scream. 'I thought you were going to –'

But just at that moment, his gaze dropped from the preacher's hatband to his burning eyes.

Cruncher felt those eyes scorching into his skull. Their power was irresistible. Their fanatical glare was scrambling his brain.

'I hate . . .' Cruncher began saying in a woozy voice. 'I hate . . .'

Then he felt something scrabbling at his shoe, looked down for a second.

'*Aaaargh!*' It was Claw, climbing up his trouser leg. 'Gerroff! Gerroff me!' cried Cruncher.

He didn't know that the grim-looking metal gauntlet only needed love and protection. It needed a Mummy Claw. And it had chosen Cruncher.

There were lots of things about Cruncher that weren't Mummy-like. Or even Claw-like – only his dagger thumb fitted the bill. But to tell the truth, Claw wasn't all that bright. Crisp-making robots don't have to be. And besides that, it was desperate. Any Mummy would do.

But already, Cruncher's eyes had slipped

back to Silas Smite's. And this time, he couldn't tear them away. He forgot about Claw. Forgot his own name, as the preacher's poison poured into his mind.

'You hate potatoes,' said Silas Smite. 'And all their products.'

'I hate potatoes,' repeated Cruncher, obediently. 'And all their products.' Cruncher began to chant a list of forbidden foods. 'That means waffles, micro chips, straight, crinkly and mega. And, and –'

Inside Cruncher's head, there was still a struggle going on. His love of crisps was so strong, he just couldn't include them. Somewhere deep in his brain, a tiny, desperate voice was crying, *No, no, I will never betray crisps!*

But one blast from Silas Smite's eyes silenced that voice.

'And crisps,' droned Cruncher, 'I hate crisps most of all.'

Just at that moment, Professor Kettles slipped in through the church door. He summed up the situation in one glance: *That monster, he's brainwashed Cruncher. He's got Claw too.*

He shrank back into the shadows so he wouldn't be seen.

'Good,' Silas Smite told Cruncher, with a nod of approval.

The preacher was pleased with his new powers. He'd always wanted to possess people's minds, force them to think like him. Back in the past, he'd gone around preaching and chopping off potato thumbnails. Peasants had repeated after him, 'We hate taters.' But in their hearts they'd never been true believers. As soon as his back was turned, they'd grown those thumbnails long again, started secretly scoffing spuds. Gone back to their sinful, potato-loving ways.

But now he could have a whole army of spud-hating fanatics, just like him.

We would be invincible, he thought. *No one would dare stand up against us.*

But for the moment, this one puny boy would have to do. He might be useful, though, in the great battle against the potato menace.

'Follow me,' Silas Smite ordered Cruncher. 'We have work to do.'

Claw was still hanging on to Cruncher's baggy trousers, its sharp talons clutching the cloth. It wasn't going to be shaken off. Not now it had found a Mummy Claw to cling to.

When Cruncher started to walk, Claw's sensitive fingers explored, found a place to hide. It sneaked into Cruncher's biggest, roomiest pocket. And curled up there into a fist. Snug as a baby kangaroo in its mother's pouch.

Cruncher would have had kittens if he'd known Claw was hitching a ride in his trousers. And thought of him as its Mummy. That robot hand gave him the creeps. But he didn't notice – he was too well hypnotized. He didn't even notice how hard it was walking with a claw in your trouser pocket.

'Potato wedges,' Cruncher was still chanting a list of sinful snacks as he trudged behind the preacher to the council tip, 'with curry sauce.'

Energy crackled through the air. The pressure was building up, like a volcano about to blow. Under the black storm clouds, the mountain tops throbbed with a vile, yellow glow.

Prof Kettles tiptoed behind, dodging from bush to bush. He didn't want to risk being spotted by Silas Smite. Those shears could do you a lot of damage. But so could his laser-beam eyes. They could turn you into a potato-hating moron.

'And cheesy potato puffballs,' trilled Cruncher. 'Beware cheesy potato puffballs. They are *evil*!'

'Do not forget baked potatoes,' spat Silas Smite. 'They are the most sinful of all.'

'Baked potatoes?' repeated Cruncher. Even his zombie voice sounded puzzled.

'Yes!' hissed Silas Smite, through gritted teeth.

The preacher whirled round. The thumb-nails in his hat glinted in the gloom. Cruncher's dagger thumbnail was right at the front. The freshest and newest trophy. But Cruncher wasn't aware of it. His mind had become a sponge, soaking up Silas Smite's potato hatred.

Cruncher shrank back. Silas Smite's eyes glittered like a viper about to strike.

'I had a sweetheart,' he said. 'My little Emily, a pure, innocent, young girl, soon to be my bride. At Christmas I took her to London, for a treat. We went ice-skating together, on the frozen Thames. We were happy as larks!'

'Beware oven chips,' warbled Cruncher.

'But then,' Silas Smite's face was twisted with bitterness, 'she was lured away from me!'

'And potato fritters,' sang Cruncher, as the preacher raged on.

'It was cold on the ice. My Emily's tiny hands were turning blue. A cry came from the riverside, "Buy my hot taters!" A wicked baked-potato seller tempted my bride. Whispered in her ear. Gave her one of his hot potatoes to warm her hands. My poor little Emily's head was turned. She ran off with that baked-potato seller.'

A great cry of pain filled the air. 'My poor little Emily!' howled Silas Smite. 'Tempted away from me! By a baked potato!'

Ever since then, Silas Smite had vowed revenge on the vegetable that had ruined his happiness.

He thundered from pulpits, 'I am doing God's work. Waging war on the evil potato.' But God was just an excuse. The Rev's potato hatred was purely personal.

Thinking of Emily, his lost bride, made him even more eager for what was to come. It would be an epic battle.

Silas Smite and Cruncher marched

through the great metal gates of the council tip. Professor Kettles crept in afterwards.

'Rejoice!' said Silas Smite to Cruncher, his faithful follower. 'Soon the Demon Potato will be no more!'

Chapter Ten

Deep among the garbage mountains, Grandad was still searching for space junk. Last night, he'd seen it crashland somewhere on the tip. He still had no idea it was a potato growth chamber from a space shuttle.

Maybe it's some kind of space tool, he thought.

Lots of tools floated away from astronauts on space walks – screwdrivers, wrenches, stuff like that.

He plodded up and down the stinking rubbish slopes. He didn't know that, under his feet, where chemicals met and mingled, shoots were writhing and Space Potatoes were swelling. Or that, out of sight, in a canyon between the garbage mountains, the mother plant had caught its sixth seagull. Plus three black rats. Now it was searching for bigger prey.

Grandad shivered.

Strange weather, he thought.

That summer storm was taking a long time to pass. Every few seconds, lightning flashes lit up the tip. Gave him glimpses of JCBs, like slumbering monsters. Or potato lagoons, glinting like silver mirrors. Then everything was plunged back into gloom.

He should be running for cover, back to the caravan. It wasn't only the lightning. It was that creepy feeling of something lurking –

Grandad tried to deny it: 'Don't be daft. It's just a storm. It'll blow over.'

He carried on searching. He'd always had an obsession with space junk. He thought it should all be cleaned up. That's why he was converting an old bin van in his top-secret shed. But his flying bin van, like Scavenger Worms, had hit a few snags. Until he'd perfected it, picking up one piece of space junk here on Earth would have to do.

Besides, he was really curious to know what had landed. It might even be something big, like a rocket tailfin.

Cruncher would be really impressed, he thought.

But something big, when it slammed into the ground, would have left a scorched crater

– maybe even one the size of a football pitch. Surely he'd have found that by now?

He toiled up yet another garbage mountain. Even Grandad was beginning to lose heart.

Then he caught sight of something out of the corner of his eye. Something squirming above the top of a garbage mountain.

Grandad stared, bewildered. What on Earth was it? It was so gloomy up there with the low black clouds pressing down, it was hard to see.

Then the lightning flashed. In the blue glow Grandad saw a snaky tentacle. Like a giant squid, except it was leafy. It uncurled and waved about triumphantly.

'What *is* that?' muttered Grandad. He was talking to himself, he didn't expect an answer. But then a voice, as shocked as his own, replied: 'It's the Space Potato. It survived the journey.'

'Professor!' said Grandad. 'Where did you spring from?'

The Professor didn't say that he'd been tailing Cruncher, Silas Smite and Claw. But had lost sight of them just moments ago, among the rubbish mountains. That went out of his head temporarily. He was so staggered, so totally gobsmacked by what he saw.

'What a magnificent specimen!' said Professor Kettles, as they both stared upwards. 'I knew it would be something special. Something totally unknown to science. But I never dreamed . . .'

'What did you say it was?' interrupted Grandad, as more bushy arms waved above the mountain top.

'It's a potato plant,' said Professor Kettles.

'You're joking,' said Grandad. But, he should have known, Professor Kettles never, *ever*, joked about potatoes.

'Let's take a closer look,' said the Prof.

He'd forgotten that Grandad hadn't heard the latest news. As they scrambled round the mountain for a better view, the Prof, in a few breathless words, brought Grandad up to date on Space Potatoes.

'So you're telling me that *thing* was growing inside the space junk?' said Grandad. 'And even the crash didn't kill it? It must be indestructible!'

'Well, they *were* trying to breed a new, tougher plant,' the Professor reasoned.

'Don't you think they went a bit too far?' said Grandad.

But it was only when they got to the other

side of their garbage mountain, that they appreciated the full, heart-stopping horror of the super spud.

'It's a monster!' breathed Grandad.

It was rooted in the opposite slope. But it almost covered the garbage mountain it was growing on. Its forest of snaky branches reached to the sky. And it was moving, like giant seaweed in a stormy sea. Its leafy arms were squirming, wriggling, in constant, restless motion.

'It's alive!' said Grandad.

'Course it's alive. But it's only a plant,' said Professor Kettles, although he sounded a bit doubtful about that.

Then Grandad saw something else. At the bottom of the space spud's garbage mountain were two tiny figures.

'That's Cruncher,' said Grandad. 'Cruncher! It's me!' he bellowed, loud enough to wake the dead.

But Cruncher didn't even turn round. Had he gone deaf?

Who's he with? thought Grandad. He strained his eyes, trying to see.

And suddenly a ray of light found its way between the storm clouds. It was pale and feeble but strong enough for Grandad to get a better view. He didn't like what he saw. Cruncher's companion was a spidery, black-clad figure wearing a battered straw hat, like a scarecrow.

'Who *is* that guy?' Grandad asked the Prof, urgently. 'What's Cruncher doing with him?'

But Prof Kettles was busy studying the Space Potato.

'Oh dear,' he said. 'I think that potato's intelligent.'

'What?' said Grandad. He was hardly listening. He was desperately trying to work out what Cruncher and the sinister scarecrow were doing. Hadn't he always told Cruncher never, ever to go off with strangers?

'I think it's intelligent,' repeated the Prof. 'But there's worse news than that.'

He'd just spotted that the Space Potato, like a macabre Christmas tree, was decorated with corpses. There were seagulls, dozens of them. And some brown furry things he couldn't identify. Their shrivelled bodies hung from the giant plant's sticky branches.

'What news?' said Grandad, tearing his attention away from his grandson.

'I think,' said Professor Kettles, 'that it's carnivorous.'

'What are you saying?' Grandad just couldn't take it in. 'It sounds like something out of a horror film!'

'Not at all,' argued Prof Kettles, as if Grandad shouldn't be surprised.

'We already have carnivorous plants. And plants with simple nervous systems, even memories. Take the Venus flytrap, for instance. This plant, it's just a bit more advanced. And bigger –'

As he spoke, the Space Potato writhed in the electrically charged air. Its rustling branches hissed like a nest of monster snakes. It seemed to be sucking in energy. Growing stronger.

'You mean it kills things?' said Grandad, still not understanding.

'Watch,' said Professor Kettles.

The Space Potato had suddenly curled up, gone quiet. A crow, black as the storm clouds, came flapping over.

The Space Potato pounced. *Sssss*. A sticky stem whiplashed out, wrapped itself around the crow. Tightened.

'What's it doing?' cried Grandad, horrified.

'It's squeezing it to death,' said Prof Kettles.

The branches were squirming again, as if eager for their dinner. The crow was drawn down into the thrashing mass.

'What's it doing now?' cried Grandad, hardly able to believe his eyes.

'It's digesting it, sucking out the nutritious juices. Soon the crow will be a dried-up husk.'

'That's disgusting!' said Grandad.

'No, no,' insisted Prof Kettles. 'It's nature. Lots of carnivorous plants do it. They digest their prey with enzymes . . .'

'I don't want a biology lesson,' said Grandad, getting more and more agitated. 'What I want to know is, it obviously wouldn't be interested in *people*, would it?'

'*Well* . . .' began Prof Kettles.

'Just say it wouldn't,' begged Grandad.

'I can't be sure. Science has never seen . . .'

'Let's get Cruncher out of there!'

Grandad was already clambering down the garbage mountain.

'Wait!' said Prof Kettles.

'There's no time to wait!' said Grandad. You could feel it in the air. It had been building up for days. The tension was at breaking point.

'*Great forces colliding, critical mass,*' murmured Professor Kettles, grimly.

'What are you talking about? Come on!' cried Grandad.

'Wait!' insisted Prof Kettles, grabbing hold of Grandad's baggy jumper. 'Wait. You don't know what you're taking on. There are some things you need to know about Silas Smite.'

'Who?' said Grandad.

'Silas Smite, the rabid potato-hating fanatic who's captured Cruncher.'

Chapter Eleven

Claw stuck a silver talon out of Cruncher's trouser pocket. It was feeling bolder. Now it had Mummy Claw to come back to, it didn't mind exploring a bit.

Claw scuttled down Cruncher's leg. Began crawling round in the smelly mud, like a curious baby. Thinking for itself was scary. But another feeling was buzzing through Claw's circuits. It was excitement – at being out on its own; at not having to take orders from anyone.

Nobody noticed it, down at ground level, learning about the big wide world, getting more confident all the time. Prof Kettles and Grandad were too far away. Cruncher was zombified – the main thought in his head was, *I hate potatoes*. Silas Smite was too busy sharpening those giant-sized shears on a rock.

Kkkkkkk: the grating sound set your teeth on edge.

Even if anyone had noticed Claw, they would probably have screamed, '*Ugh!* Get that horrible thing away from me.'

No one understood Claw. No one dreamed that inside that brutal-looking metal gauntlet was a sensitive touchy-feely creature trying to work out how the world worked and where claws fitted in.

And Claw, in its turn, didn't understand what was happening above mud level, that warfare was about to break out, that if Silas Smite won, or the Space Potato, the world it was just starting to learn about would never be the same again.

Claw scuttled about, never straying too far from its adopted Mummy.

Silas Smite gazed up at his arch-enemy, the Space Potato. His rage made him super powerful. He seemed to be swelling, getting bigger. A fire was burning inside him. Flames danced in his eyes.

He waved his shears above his head. A lightning bolt hissed down. Blue sparks danced around the blades. 'I am going to get thee, Demon!' roared Silas Smite at the Space

Potato. His voice vibrated through the air.

The Space Potato seemed to feel it. It stopped digesting the seagull. Its branches curled. The whole plant was still, suspecting danger.

Down on the ground, Claw sensed the bad vibrations too. It didn't understand about evil. But something made it drop the rusty baked-bean can it was playing with. *Whirr, click*, it flopped over and played dead. Then it thought of a better idea. It flipped back and scuttled up into Cruncher's baggies. But not without snatching the tin can to take with it.

Safe, its primitive robot brain told it, as it snuggled back into Mummy's pouch. With its razor-sharp talons, it began shredding the baked-bean can into thin strips. To make cosy bedding for its nest.

The Space Potato also had a primitive brain. Like Claw, it knew when it was being threatened. But unlike Claw, it didn't play dead. Electrical surges, like thoughts, passed down its sticky branches: *Attack! Attack!*

Silas Smite clashed his shears, shrieked his war cry: 'Vengeance is mine!'

Those evil tentacles would soon be hacked

123

to pieces. He knew he had the power. That wouldn't be the end of it – even now the children of the sinful Space Potato were swelling under the ground. But his army of followers would soon dig those up, destroy them. Silas Smite had big plans. He would make every child, every adult, forget their families, their friends, their homes. Even their own names. Everyone would think alike.

A whole nation, a whole world, of potato smiters.

It had always been his dream.

He thought, *I will be their leader. They shall obey me without question.*

The thumbnail trophies in his hat blazed out, as if he was wearing a fiery crown.

But first he had to deal with his rival for world domination. He needed a little diversion. Something to distract it. So he could sneak up, surprise it and slice it to bits.

'You! Peasant!'

Cruncher's eyes, when he stared up at Silas Smite, were blank. Except for two tiny twin reflections of the preacher.

'Yes, Master,' said Cruncher.

'Now is your chance for glory!' raved Silas Smite. 'To redeem your wicked, potato-loving past. Do you see the Demon Potato?'

The preacher pointed with a quivering arm.

Cruncher gazed at the Space Potato. It waved above the top of the garbage mountain. Its sticky, strangling arms were thrashing about, hissing like cobras. But Cruncher's face showed no fear. Just total obedience.

'Go thou and smite it!' ordered the preacher.

'Yes, Master.'

Stiffly, like a soldier, Cruncher marched towards the garbage mountain. Claw was curled up in its pouch, feeling safe and snug. It had no idea that momentous events were taking place all around it, that what happened today on the council tip could change the course of history. Instead it was planning another little trip – not too far away from Mummy, though. Just to rootle round in the dirt. See if it could find some more exciting treasures, like the baked-bean can, to bring back to its den.

Another new feeling fizzed through Claw's circuits. For the first time in its life, the metal fist felt something very much like happiness.

From the other garbage mountain, Grandad watched, appalled.

'He's sending Cruncher up there!'

Grandad began slithering, sliding down the side of the garbage mountain. 'Cruncher!' he bellowed. But Cruncher didn't even turn his head. Just kept his eyes locked on the Demon Potato. Master had given him his mission. To smite the evil potato, mightily.

'He's heading straight for it!' cried Grandad. 'What's wrong with the boy? Can't he see it's dangerous!'

'I told you,' said Prof Kettles, panting behind him. 'He can't help it. He's been brainwashed.'

'That Silas Smite!' cried Grandad. 'He'd better watch out. Wait until I get hold of him!'

Grandad heaved an old fridge freezer out of his way. His bulky body came charging down the slope like an angry old grizzly bear.

Prof Kettles got his trousers hooked on a rusty iron spring. He stopped to untangle himself. He'd never catch up with Grandad now.

'Remember!' he shouted after him. 'Don't look into his eyes. Whatever you do, don't look into his eyes!'

*

The Space Potato knew Cruncher was approaching. It couldn't see him. But it could feel the heat of his body, sense his footsteps. And it knew he was something big and meaty. A much better dinner than a seagull or a rat. It rustled its great, swarming branches in greedy excitement.

Sssss!

Then it went quiet and crouched, waiting for the right moment to spring. Cruncher was its first human prey.

The whole council tip seemed to go quiet too. The air was still. The torn carrier bags stopped blowing about like tumbleweed. The light, already murky, went darker.

'I hate micro chips – crinkly and straight and mega. And cheesy potato puffballs and crisps.'

As Cruncher reached the lower slopes of the garbage mountain, a chirpy little spud-hating song filled the silence. He wasn't singing to keep his courage up. He wasn't aware he was about to be eaten. He was just following Master's orders.

'Smite the Demon Potato,' he warbled.

Except it was a bit tricky to know where to start.

The monster plant loomed above Cruncher. Like Jack's beanstalk, it seemed to vanish into the clouds. At first its leafy arms dazzled you. They sparkled with sticky droplets like millions of tiny mirrors.

You might even have thought, *How beautiful!*

But if you looked closer you saw the gruesome truth. Those gluey droplets held withered bodies, some furry, some feathered. They were the Space Potato's prey, sucked dry. All their blood and other nutritious juices had been slowly absorbed by the plant.

Cruncher looked back down the slope for further instructions from his master. But Silas Smite was nowhere to be seen.

A whippy branch shot out, like an octopus tentacle. Writhed along the ground towards Cruncher. With a quick flick, the tip looped around his ankle, yanked him off his feet. Before Cruncher could even cry out, he was dangling upside down, held fast by one leg.

'No!' yelled Grandad, who was down in the deep, dark valley between one garbage mountain and another.

Cruncher was swung high in the air. Carried towards the bushiest part of the plant where many green sticky arms waited to wrap him up like a fly in a spider's web. Then the digesting process could begin.

Click, whirr. Claw felt its cosy den turning topsy-turvy. It put its long silver talons out of Cruncher's knee pocket. What was happening to Mummy? Claw was shaken out of its nest. Frantically, it clutched Cruncher's trousers to stop itself falling. Something was trying to separate it from Mummy Claw! Its circuits went into stress overload.

'Do not forget baked potatoes,' sang Cruncher as he was swung in the air like a pendulum. 'They are the most evil of all.' He didn't seem to have a clue what was going on. Only Claw was panicking.

It felt something alien wrapped around Mummy. The Space Potato radiated bad vibrations. Claw lashed out with its deadly crisp-making talons. Jabbed the branch that held Cruncher prisoner. The Space Potato knew instantly it was under attack. The wounded branch uncoiled like a spring.

Both Cruncher and Claw were catapulted away from the plant. Grandad saw his grandson sailing through the air. If he'd been closer, he might have heard Cruncher warble, as he

shot by overhead, 'And potato waffles are wicked!'

From somewhere in the gloom came a distant *plosh*.

He's fallen in a potato lagoon! thought Grandad.

At least it was a soft landing – that potato sludge was like porridge. But it sucked you under, even quicker if you struggled.

Grandad had almost reached the Space Potato. But now he swerved round, intending to rush down the mountain to fish Cruncher out. There wasn't much time . . .

A voice close to Grandad's ear cut through his frantic thoughts.

It said, 'Look into my eyes, peasant.'

Grandad turned, saw a granite face, searing eyes under a scarecrow hat. Rows of thumbnails, one of which, although he didn't know it, was his own grandson's.

It's Silas Smite, thought Grandad. *Don't look into his eyes.*

But by the time he'd warned himself, it was already far too late.

Chapter Twelve

Prof Kettles hadn't seen Cruncher and his own precious crisp-making machine fly past. He was still unhooking himself from the bedspring when that happened. But now he was free. And he'd almost caught up with Grandad. He had his best view yet of the Space Potato.

Amazing, he thought, his goggly eyes gleaming.

As a potato boffin, he couldn't help being impressed. It was a spectacular specimen. As different from an ordinary spud as a shark from a sardine.

He crept towards it. Then he saw the burly figure of Grandad, standing next to Silas Smite like an obedient dog.

He could hear Grandad's growly voice. What was he chanting? It was his own

personal list of forbidden potato foods: 'Mash, roasties – they are wicked!'

'Oh no,' groaned Professor Kettles. Silas Smite had got himself another convert.

'Potatoes are the Devil's vegetable,' boomed Grandad.

His voice echoed eerily round the garbage mountains: *Devil's vegetable, Devil's vegetable*. Scared, a flock of crows clattered into the sky. The Space Potato flung out all its sticky arms, trying to snatch them as they flew by. For a few seconds, it was off guard.

Silas Smite saw his chance. It was his moment of glory. He screamed, 'Attack! Attack!'

He waved his shears above his head. Pointed them at the evil invader: 'Charge!'

He and Grandad pounded towards the Space Potato. But already its snaky branches were wriggling along the ground to meet Grandad. It sensed its biggest meal yet. Compared to Grandad, crows and even Cruncher would have been just a light snack.

Prof Kettles yelled out in despair, 'No, come back.'

He started forwards. Perhaps he could grab Grandad, wrestle him to the ground. But even running full pelt, Silas Smite still found time to turn his head.

Prof Kettles shrank back. 'His eyes, his eyes,' he groaned, covering his face with his hands.

He heard the Space Potato hissing. Had it got Grandad? Was it squeezing the life out of him? Before feasting on his bodily fluids?

He had to see what was happening. He peeped through his fingers.

A child was standing between the two charging adults and the Space Potato. A tiny, frail child whose bare feet were frosty blue with cold and whose dress looked like an old coal sack . . .

'It's the Little Waif,' gasped Professor Kettles.

She looked so fragile. She'd get trampled by the grown-ups. The Space Potato would strangle her in two seconds. A sticky stem sneaked towards her.

'Get out of there!' screamed Professor Kettles, frantically waving his arms.

But the Little Waif didn't budge. She stood her ground. The radiance around her grew even brighter.

And the Space Potato stem, almost at her

133

throat, drew back: *Ssss*, as if it had touched a hot stove.

And then an even weirder thing happened. The preacher was foaming at the mouth with potato hatred. He was all fired up to fight. When, suddenly, in mid-screech, he froze like a statue, with his shears above his head.

Prof Kettles thought, *What's going on?*

Grandad, charging beside him, had stopped dead too. Caught on one leg like a ballet dancer. Then even the monster plant was struck motionless. Its writhing arms seemed turned to stone.

It was as though someone had pressed a pause button. Or cast a stillness spell. But, somehow, the Little Waif wasn't affected.

She turned to Professor Kettles, beckoned him.

'Come hither, sir. Silas Smite will not hurt you.'

Prof Kettles found he still had the use of his limbs. He crept warily forwards. The Little Waif was right. Silas Smite didn't even glance at him. He was frozen where he stood. Even his laser-beam eyes didn't seem dangerous now. They were dim, like shaded lamps.

As Prof Kettles faced the Little Waif, he

saw who had the real strength. It was the one who seemed to have none. Who seemed to be the weakest and most helpless of them all.

A halo of white light surrounded her, like a defence shield. Her eyes, huge as a bush-baby's, gazed directly into his. They were clear and calm.

Professor Kettles felt humbled. This puny little child looked like a puff of wind could blow her away. But she somehow possessed great power. He was convinced that she was in control of what was happening. That she had stopped Silas Smite in his tracks. Even tamed the wild and savage Space Potato.

He said, respectfully, 'Who are you?'

'I be from Robin's Corner,' she told him. 'I be Jane Shore.'

'Jane Shore?'

The Professor searched his memory. His mind was stuffed with potato facts – he didn't have much room for other things. But even he'd heard of the great fire of Robin's Corner. And the evil child who was supposed to have started it. She'd been a hate figure for almost three hundred years. Since the eighteenth century, little kids had had nightmares about her. They'd woken up screaming, 'Mother!

Don't let Jane Shore burn *us* in our beds!'

His brain couldn't cope with this. From weak, to powerful, to wicked – just what *was* the truth about this child?

'*You're* Jane Shore!' said the Professor, shaking his head in disbelief. 'But weren't you the wicked child who . . .?'

He felt a tiny hand, like a bundle of twigs, slide into his. 'Sir,' said Jane Shore. 'I be here to right a great wrong. You shall see the truth. With your own eyes.'

And in an instant he was whisked away on a journey. The world whirled around him. He felt himself travelling, dragged backwards, as if through a long tunnel . . .

'Where am I?' Professor Kettles stared about him, stunned.

The council tip had vanished. So had the Space Potato.

Instead, he was in some kind of wretched, smoky hovel. With a dirt floor and walls made out of mud and sticks. The walls had cracks in, where the wind blew through.

There were other people here – he could see them, huddled in the shadows. The only light was from a feeble fire.

He'd said, 'Where am I?' out loud. But no one seemed to have heard it. No one jumped out of their skin, or shouted, 'Who are you?' They looked straight through him. As if he was made of air.

Professor Kettles was still shell-shocked, after his swirling journey. But he wasn't totally surprised. It was all part of the general chaos. What was happening at the tip broke all the rules of space – and time. As he'd already warned Cruncher, 'Expect *anything*.'

And one part of his brain wasn't scrambled. The scientific part – it stayed sharp. It looked around, curiously. Recording every detail, as if it was taking notes of an experiment.

They were a peasant family, miserably poor. Three ragged children crouched round the fire. They had bare feet like Jane Shore. They stuck their grimy toes into the warm ashes.

What was that? There was something crawling on the muddy floor! Prof Kettles peered down. It was the toad who shared the house with the family. He liked it in here, it was so damp. He flopped across the room. No one stopped him. They didn't seem to have the energy to lift their heads. Besides, Mr

Toad was useful. He ate all the cockroaches and slugs. There! He shot out his long sticky tongue. His golden eyes bulged as he gulped a slug down.

What was happening? The children seemed to be perking up. They were looking into a cooking pot on the fire.

'Mother,' said the biggest boy, 'isn't supper ready? The water is almost boiled away.'

A stooping woman came into the circle of firelight. The Professor hadn't noticed her before. She had a grey shawl wrapped round her body, pulled over her head. She poked at something in the pot with a long stick.

Professor Kettles crept forwards. He didn't need to creep really. He'd already deduced that he was invisible here. Just a watcher. Or even, perhaps, a witness. There was something Jane Shore wanted him to see.

He couldn't help thinking, *She looked so innocent.*

But Jane Shore burned a village down. Almost no one escaped. The old rhyme said it was her; it was in all the history books. Everyone knew she was to blame.

'Come, children,' said the mother, lifting the pot.

The children scurried to their table – a rough bit of tree trunk. The mother tipped out the supper, straight on to the table.

'Potatoes,' murmured Prof Kettles.

They were still in their skins. And then the Professor saw that the whole family, mother and children, had potato thumbs.

'I loves taters, Mother!' said the smallest.

'*Shhh!*' said the mother, looking over her shoulder. '*Shhh! He* might hear you!'

She hurried to the door, looked out, came back. Why were they all so afraid? '*Shhh!*' she said again. 'Be silent!'

They had no knives, or spoons, or plates. They scraped the skin off the potatoes with their long, sharp thumbnails. The mother smashed the spuds with her fist, right there, on the table. 'Eat,' she said.

The children fell on the spuds like wolves, shovelling them in, even though they were still too hot.

'Elijah Shore,' said the mother. 'You will burn your mouth.'

Shore? thought Professor Kettles. *Surely that couldn't be a coincidence?*

Then the mother said, 'Save some for Jane.'

That settled it: *I'm in Robin's Corner. This is*

Jane Shore's family. Prof Kettles had already suspected it. He'd been taken back through time. *But where was Jane?*

The Professor looked round. It was then that he saw the eyes spying at the peasant family through a crack in the wall.

They weren't Jane Shore's eyes.

'Oh no!' Professor Kettles shielded his own eyes. He waited for anti-spud slogans to invade his brain. They didn't.

Slowly, he uncovered his eyes, dared to take another look. It was Silas Smite all right. He'd recognize those eyes anywhere, burning with hatred and gleeful spite, because he'd sniffed out some poor peasants to punish.

But the preacher's eyes didn't seem to have the same brainwashing powers.

Phew, thought Prof Kettles. *That's a relief.*

This Silas Smite seemed like a pussycat compared to his twenty-first-century reincarnation.

But Prof Kettles was just about to discover how wrong he was.

The door of the hovel burst open: 'Sinners!' All the spud eaters looked up, their eyes wide with horror.

'Sir!' pleaded the mother. 'This is our only

food. My children will starve! They have no father to provide for them.'

But Silas Smite was merciless. He never listened to excuses. 'Show me your thumbs!'

Then *Schwack! Schwack!* The iron shears snapped, four times. Silas Smite scooped up the thumbnails and stuck them in his hatband. He swept their potato supper on to the floor and stomped it into the dirt. The children started crying. The littlest scrabbled in the dirt, cramming mashed spud and mud into her mouth.

'You big bully!' yelled Professor Kettles. 'Leave them alone!'

No one even turned to look at him. He might have been whispering in the wind.

Silas Smite hadn't finished yet. He'd just seen something even more sinful than having potatoes for supper. He quivered with righteous anger.

'Your roof!' he thundered, his scorching eyes gazing upwards. 'It is made of the stalks of potato plants. You know that is forbidden!'

The mother gasped. 'Sir!' She fell to her knees and seized Silas Smite's coat-tails. 'Sir, forgive us. My husband is dead. We are poor. We cannot afford straw.'

But it was like asking a stone to feel pity.

Silas Smite poked at the roof with his shears. But that didn't bring it down fast enough. Then he had a better idea. He sprang over to the fire. Took out a burning twig.

Professor Kettles couldn't believe it. He lunged forwards. 'No, you maniac!'

He meant to grab Silas Smite, stop him from burning the house down. But he just couldn't make contact. He seemed to flow around Silas Smite's body like water. Now he was watching him from the other side.

Silas Smite thrust the fiery stick into the roof. A spark took hold. It glowed brighter, redder. While the family cowered on the floor beneath him, Silas Smite took off his scare-crow hat, fanned the spark.

That seemed to do the job. A tiny flame danced. More flickered into life – orange, yellow, crimson. They gobbled up the potato-stalk roof with terrible speed.

'Get out! Get out!' shrieked Prof Kettles to the terrified family. But no one heard.

Silas Smite nodded in satisfaction. Pulled his hat back on, whisked out of the door with his black coat-tails flapping.

'Better no roof,' he roared back over his

shoulder, 'than a roof of the Devil's root!'

He crashed into Jane Shore, on her way in.

'Mother!' she was shouting. 'Elijah!'

She'd been out collecting firewood. The force of the collision with Silas Smite threw her backwards. She tumbled on to the ground, hit her head on a rock. Sticks scattered all around her.

Silas Smite stepped over her: 'Out of my way, girl!' How long had she been there? Had she seen what had happened?

Then he was off, legging it towards the church. Even for him, he'd gone too far – the Bishop wouldn't be pleased. He was already wondering how to shift the blame.

The hovel was filling with black smoke. Why didn't the family run? They huddled, still frozen with fear, on the ground. Now, Prof Kettles couldn't see them through the swirling smoke. But he could hear them coughing. He knew the fumes would choke them, long before the flames reached them.

'Get out! Get out!' His helplessness was making him frantic.

But then the scene changed. Prof Kettles found himself with a bird's-eye view, gazing down at the doomed village.

The hovel he'd been in was completely alight. No one came running out of the door. 'Oh no,' groaned Professor Kettles, hovering just overhead. He knew there was no hope for the family.

But now others were in danger too. The flames were spreading, leaping like flying squirrels from one hovel's roof to another.

This time, the Professor didn't shout out. He knew they couldn't hear him. Even if they could, he was up here, just under the clouds, far too far away.

Above him, the clouds flushed rosy pink with the sunset. But he didn't notice. He couldn't take his eyes off Robin's Corner and the terrible story unfolding down on the ground.

Jane Shore staggered up. Tried to rush into her burning home to rescue her family. Flames caught her dress, she fell back and beat them out with her hands. Rushed in a second time. But the heat and smoke drove her out. She fell sobbing on the ground.

The rest of the village was blazing now. The flames were roaring and crackling. As the sky reflected the fire, the pink blush around Professor Kettles became deep, blood red.

Looking down, he saw a few coughing figures stagger out of the houses and collapse outside. But not many. Not many.

Then he was whisked away again. And this time, Prof Kettles found himself in his own factory. But there were pews here instead of crisp-making machines.

I'm still in the eighteenth century, thought Professor Kettles. He was the silent watcher in the back row. Invisible and helpless. It was torture.

But the Professor had to accept that he wasn't here to change history. Jane Shore had sent him through time for another reason. To prove she didn't start the fire. To let him see with his own eyes who was really guilty.

But there must be something more she wanted to show him.

'This is important!' Prof Kettles told himself. He struggled to concentrate. To drive the nightmare scenes he'd just witnessed out of his mind.

The few survivors of the great fire had taken shelter in the church. It was the only building left standing.

But instead of giving them comfort, Silas Smite was up in the pulpit preaching one of his hate-filled sermons. His voice echoed through the church. Made the poor, shocked survivors shake even more.

But, for once, the sermon didn't seem to be about potatoes.

The preacher's quivering finger pointed straight to the back of the church, to the very pew where Prof Kettles was sitting.

'There is the wicked wretch!' he thundered.

Does he mean me? thought the Professor. His heart gave a panicky flutter. He had to remind himself he was invisible.

Then he saw that, further down the pew, half hidden in shadow, was a heap of rags. It moved. It lifted its tear-streaked face. It was Jane Shore.

'I saw thee, Jane Shore,' screamed Silas Smite, his whole body shaking. 'I saw thee, monster! You were carrying sticks. You set the fire!'

The sad group of survivors turned to stare at her. Their eyes were red and watery with smoke and weeping. Could she really be guilty? Some were doubtful. But others already believed it – they needed someone to blame.

Jane Shore opened her mouth like a baby

bird. She tried to protest, 'I am innocent! I would not harm my mother, my sister and brothers!'

But Silas Smite was already dealing with that.

'And why, I hear you say, did she do this foul deed? Why did she set fire to her own village? The answer is simple! See her potato thumb!'

Professor Kettles groaned. He'd guessed Silas Smite would bring in potatoes before long.

'That is proof,' the preacher raved on, 'that she is the servant of the evil potato! The Devil's root whispers in her ear: *Burn down Robin's Corner*. And she obeys! She shows no mercy. Even for her own mother!'

The Professor thought, *For heaven's sake. A potato told her to burn down the village? They'll never swallow that.*

But they did. They were driven almost mad by grief and terror. They hardly knew what they were doing. 'Monster!' shouted one. 'Murderer!' said another.

'And,' shrieked Silas Smite, doing some more rabble-rousing, 'I saw her! Yea, nothing escapes my eye! I saw her use that wicked thumb to start the fire. Strike it on a stone until it made a spark! I tried in vain to save her family. But the flames were too strong!'

Some were already running towards the back of the church. Others followed.

'See, did I not warn you about potatoes?' said Silas Smite, smugly. 'They are the source of all evil.'

He smiled as the survivors turned into a screaming mob.

He whipped up their hatred a bit more. He leaned out from the pulpit, right over the eagle's outspread wings.

'Hunt her down!' he roared, *schwacking* his iron shears. 'The wicked wretch. She burns houses to the ground! Let loose the biggest hound! Hunt her down!'

As the survivors trampled towards her, Jane Shore rose in her pew. Over the heads of the mob, she gave Silas Smite a single, sorrowful glance. It only lasted a second. But it seemed to make the preacher cringe back, shrivel up in the pulpit, like a slug sprinkled with salt.

Prof Kettles thought, astonished, *He's scared of her*.

But he recovered almost immediately. So

quickly that the Professor thought he'd been mistaken.

'Hunt her down!' shrieked Silas Smite, in a frenzy.

'Run!' said the Professor to Jane Shore. 'Run for your life!'

But the girl was already gone. She'd slipped out of the church door. The howling mob ran after her.

Would they catch her? The Professor rushed to the church door.

He saw the mob racing over the moors in the fiery sunset. But where was their quarry? He couldn't see Jane anywhere.

The mob's voices faded into the distance. Jane Shore crawled out from beneath a heather bush. She'd given them the slip.

With his heart aching Professor Kettles watched her, a tiny forlorn figure, walk off down the dirt road until she disappeared from view.

Then the eighteenth century suddenly swirled around him. He put a hand to his spinning head. He knew by now what was happening. He was being taken back to the twenty-first century. Jane Shore had finished telling her story.

'But the story *isn't* finished!' protested Professor Kettles, as he felt his feet on firm ground. 'What happened to her after she escaped? Where did she go?'

He opened his eyes. He was back on the council tip. Halfway up a garbage mountain.

And the great enemies were still immobilized. Prof Kettles sighed with relief. Silas Smite was stuck in mid-charge, with Grandad beside him. The Space Potato's arms were frozen, in weird, twisted shapes.

And Jane Shore stood between them. Tiny, wren-like, but with a radiant light around her.

This was no time to be fretting about the past. When there were earth-shattering events happening here, in the present. But Prof Kettles just had to tell Jane Shore something.

'I know the truth,' he told her. 'I know who burned down Robin's Corner.'

Jane Shore nodded and smiled. It was the first time the Professor had seen her smile.

He was going to say: 'I'm so sorry about your family.' To ask her, 'What happened to you, after the fire? Where did you go?'

He had to know, although he dreaded the answer. Who would take her in, after Silas

Smite's sermon? She could have starved to death, died in a ditch.

But he never got the chance to ask his questions. From the clouds overhead came a sizzling bolt of lightning. It slammed into the garbage mountain. Electric shocks spread out like waves. Prof Kettles felt his hair frizzle.

Silas Smite's eyes, so lifeless and dull, suddenly clicked on again, like headlight beams. His shears clashed, *SCHWACK*, with renewed energy.

From the Space Potato came an ominous hiss.

If Prof Kettles thought the battle had been postponed, or even cancelled, he was living in dreamland.

Battle was about to commence.

Chapter Thirteen

Cruncher floated on his back in a potato lagoon. He wasn't panicking. He seemed quite calm, as if he was relaxing in a swimming pool on holiday. He didn't even seem to notice the dreadful stench. He just stared up at the clouds, chanting his little anti-potato song.

He warbled, 'I hate waffles and crisps. And Potato Alphabites are wicked.' That was a new forbidden food he'd added. He'd never eaten them, but he'd seen them in the freezer at the supermarket.

It was a good job he was zombified. If he'd struggled, he'd have been sucked down by now.

But he was still in grave danger. When he'd landed, he'd smashed through the cheesy green crust. Now he was spread out, like a starfish, on the grey porridge of potato sludge. At first, it had supported him, like a cushion. It was even quite comfy. But it was treacherous. Because, all the while, it was soaking his clothes, seeping into the pockets of his baggies. Soon it would drag him down into the depths.

Only Claw was aware that this was an emergency.

As Cruncher sailed through the air, Claw had clung on grimly. When Cruncher landed, *splosh*, in the potato lagoons, Claw had hidden at first in its pocket den. Then it had crept out to explore.

Mummy Claw had become an island, surrounded by a sludgy sea.

Claw scuttled up to Cruncher's head, dipped a silver talon in the quaking potato bog. Its sensors told it: *Danger*. It scuttled down to Cruncher's trainer, explored again.

Danger everywhere.

And all the time, Cruncher lay, crooning his little anti-spud song. Completely unaware that he was slowly being sucked down by a potato bog and that he had a robot hand scuttling up and down his body like a giant silver spider.

Claw had been depending on the protection of Mummy Claw. To help it get used to its new life, in the big scary world outside the factory.

But now Mummy Claw wasn't responding. Claw's circuits buzzed with anxiety. *What to do?*

It crept up to Cruncher's face. Claw was a very touchy-feely creature. It learned about the world through its sensitive silver fingers.

Click, whirr. Claw gently stroked Cruncher's face. Brushing over it as lightly as a snowflake. Trying to find out what was wrong with him.

Cruncher didn't even say, 'That tickles.' His stony face didn't even crease up. His reaction was zero.

Claw's sensors told it: *Mummy Claw is malfunctioning!*

Claw felt lost and abandoned. As close as a crisp-making machine can come to despair. But then it started thinking for itself. It had to. It had no other choice.

Its delicate sensors, aware of every shift in its surroundings, could feel Mummy Claw sinking deeper, deeper into the sludge.

Glug. Cruncher's body jolted down, another

few centimetres. Only his nose was above the green mouldy surface. If the fumes didn't kill him, the sludge would.

Still, he didn't seem worried. Muffled words, 'Sinful, sinful,' came bubbling up from under the sludge.

But Claw was paddling in sticky goo. Its sensors were getting clogged. And Mummy Claw was disappearing! It knew it had to take action.

Claw slid off Cruncher's body. Launched out into the unknown. *Click.* The metal gaunt-let locked its thumb and first finger round Cruncher's wrist. With its other three fingers it swam through the sludge, doing a very efficient doggy-paddle. It towed Cruncher behind it, making for the shore and safety.

'Get out of there!' screamed Prof Kettles to Jane Shore.

Hadn't he said that already? But then somebody had pressed the pause button and hostilities were put on hold.

But now, the war was on again. And this time, there was no stopping it.

Just like before, as the Space Potato loomed over her, Jane Shore stood her ground.

The super spud couldn't touch her. It writhed its snaky tentacles around her. But they all shrank back. It seemed like she was taboo.

But Silas Smite had murder in his eyes. To get to the Space Potato, he would smash her down. Killing his great enemy was all he cared about.

Grandad lumbered obediently behind him. But Silas Smite was far in front.

He was almost at the monster plant. Only Jane Shore was in his way. He seemed to have superhuman strength, seemed to have swelled to nine feet tall!

He swung his shears round his head, yelled out his war cry, 'Vengeance is mine!'

Then Jane Shore looked the Reverend Smite right in the eyes.

Prof Kettles thought, *She'll be brainwashed.*

But she wasn't. And that look! It was the same one she'd given the preacher in the church, just before the mob chased her out.

Silas Smite stumbled. That look had such power. It seemed to terrify him. Even though it was pure sorrow, without even a spark of revenge or hatred.

He shielded his eyes: 'Do not look at me

like that,' he moaned. He staggered about, as if he'd been mortally wounded.

He backed into the Space Potato. *Sssssssss.* Instantly all its sticky stems were on red alert. It had got him! A tentacle coiled around his waist, others bound his legs . . .

Silas Smite put up a desperate fight. But Jane Shore's look seemed to have drained his strength. With his iron shears, he hacked at the branch that squeezed him. Cut it in two. But straightaway another one took its place. Dragged him towards the thrashing centre of the plant.

His battered straw hat fell off, rolled in the mud.

He struck out feebly with his shears. But it was as if he'd given up, knew he was defeated.

He cried out to the world, 'The Devil's vegetable is victorious! You are doomed! All doomed!'

And from that moment, he started fading. He vanished the way he had come. Instead of getting more and more solid and gaining flesh, his body became fuzzy, then transparent. Finally he disappeared, back into history. And the Space Spud was left squeezing . . . nothing.

Grandad came blundering up. 'No, don't

go near that plant,' warned Prof Kettles, grabbing him.

But there was no need. As soon as Silas Smite disappeared, his brainwashing spell was broken. Grandad was himself again. Free of spud hatred – but very confused.

'What's happening? What's this doing here?' Grandad bent down to pick up Silas Smite's straw hat. For some reason it hadn't been sucked back through time.

Thumbnails were scattered all around it – the poor, pathetic remains of all the people he'd terrorized. Grandad didn't even see them. They got trampled into the dirt under his boots.

Prof Kettles didn't immediately answer Grandad's questions. He was too busy looking round for Jane Shore. He wanted to tell her, 'It's all right. He's gone.' That mad preacher, who'd framed her for a crime she didn't commit. Made her, in this neighbourhood anyway, the most hated child in history.

But Jane Shore was gone too.

Prof Kettles stared around, bewildered. Had she gone for good? He'd wanted to ask her so much.

Sssss!

Grandad grabbed him. 'Get back!'

They both stared up at the Space Potato. With Silas Smite gone, it was triumphant. It writhed, in ceaseless motion, like a giant sea anemone. It seemed to be reaching for the stars. It was doubly deadly, as if it had taken in all Silas Smite's malevolence for itself.

'Oh dear,' said Grandad, leaping out of the way as a tentacle writhed towards him. 'What do you think it wants?'

'I think,' said Prof Kettles grimly, 'that it wants to be top species. That it sees all human beings as prey. I think,' he continued, 'that that potato wants to take over the world.'

Grandad boggled. Did a spud really have those kind of ambitions? But then he remembered something dreadful. How could it have slipped his mind?

'Cruncher!' he cried. 'He's in the potato lagoons!'

Both he and the Prof started running.

Cruncher stared round. Where was he? How had he got here?

He was standing beside a potato lagoon. He stunk to high heaven. He could hardly stand his own pong – and he was used to

pretty whiffy armpits. Besides that, he felt distinctly soggy. He scraped some potato sludge out of his hair. Stared at it, baffled.

He felt a tugging at his trouser legs. Claw was trying to attract Mummy's attention, thrilled to bits that it'd rescued her and she seemed to be in full working order.

Cruncher glanced down: '*Aaaargh!*' It was that horror-film Claw, that metal beast, trying to climb up his trousers.

'Get away from me!' howled Cruncher. He bent down, tried to pluck it off. Claw could have chopped his fingers up like potato slices. But it didn't. It just clung on and as Cruncher prised one talon off, another grasped his baggies.

'Get off me!' shrieked Cruncher. 'You monster!'

Claw didn't know what Mummy Claw was saying. But it could sense the vibrations. And it knew that they were hostile.

Cruncher stooped down again, frantically tried to yank Claw off his trouser leg. Claw felt his fingers, scanned them into its robot brain.

Immediately its circuits were thrown into chaos. It thought it had found another claw. But where was that dagger thumb it felt before? And why was it being shouted at, driven off as if it wasn't wanted?

Whirr. Click. Claw let go of Cruncher, dropped to the ground.

It had made a mistake. It didn't belong here.

Claw began crawling off, very slowly, as if it could hardly summon up the will to move. Its hunched knuckles looked like a humped back. It dragged itself along like a creature in pain.

Cruncher watched it disappear among the bedsprings and bean cans and other metal rubbish. *Good!* he thought, trying to brush himself off. 'And don't come back!' he shouted after it.

Cruncher took a few sloshing steps. The sludge had filled his trainers, his pockets. He felt like a potato lagoon on legs.

He tried to scoop some of the gunge out of his trouser pockets. In the biggest one, as well as the sludge, he found some silvery metal strips. Shredded very finely, so they curled, like wood shavings. How did they get in there?

Anxious voices cut through his bewilderment. 'Cruncher!' The voices were calling his

name. Getting louder, closer. People were searching for him!

'Cruncher!' cried Grandad, rushing out from behind a garbage mountain. He gave Cruncher a big, squelchy hug.

'How on earth did you get out of that lagoon?' asked Professor Kettles.

Cruncher looked blank. 'I can't remember.'

'Never mind,' said Grandad, 'as long as you're safe.'

Claw trundled over the council tip. There was a roll of barbed wire in its way. That was no problem. It just snipped a claw-sized door in it, with its razor-sharp talons. It dragged itself through. And continued its lonesome journey.

To find somewhere, in this strange and scary world, where claws would be welcome.

Chapter Fourteen

Back inside the caravan, Grandad was opening all the windows wide. Cruncher's potato-sludge smell made your eyes water.

Meanwhile, Prof Kettles was busy explaining that the Space Potato meant big trouble.

'It's not just one plant,' he told Grandad and Cruncher. 'It's spreading underground, perhaps for miles. Space Potatoes could pop up anywhere. And each one of those potatoes, in turn, will sprout other plants.'

He paused. It was a nightmare scenario. Soon, the Space Potato would spread throughout the world like the plague. Oceans wouldn't stop it. It could probably send shoots under the seabed. Or it would only take just one of its babies to go bobbing across the Atlantic, and, within weeks, America would be infested.

'It's already shown a keen interest in human prey,' Prof Kettles reminded them.

'You mean, it'd be going after *people*,' said Cruncher shuddering.

Prof Kettles nodded. 'No one would be safe. They grow so fast. And they're strong. They could come up through concrete, even rock. And don't forget, this potato is cunning. It'd be like guerrilla warfare. You'd never know where it was going to strike next.'

Cruncher tried to imagine it.

You'd be mooching down the street one morning, on the way to meet your mates, whistling a happy tune. You'd hear a sinister, rustling sound. And, *aaargh*, you'd get grabbed by a Space Potato that had suddenly burst up through the pavement.

'And,' added Prof Kettles, just to hammer home what a deadly species they were up against, 'they can grow practically anywhere. On rotting rubbish, for example. So, one morning, you could open your dustbin . . .'

'Care for a sausage?' said Grandad, who had some sizzling in a frying pan on his tiny stove. Cruncher nodded gratefully. A sausage somehow made things seem more normal.

Cruncher jabbed his right thumb at the

sausage. He meant to spear it with his spiky nail.

'Hey!' he said, outraged. 'My dagger thumbnail's gone! It took me ages to grow that.'

Things were coming back to him now. 'That Silas Smite guy cut it off.' He shuddered at the memory. 'Where is he, anyway?'

'You don't need to worry about him,' said Professor Kettles. 'He's history.'

Outside, unseen by all of them, someone was dumping some rubbish. It was the guy with the antlers. He'd come back, found the CLOSED sign still on the gate to Grandad's Little Kingdom, but the gates of the council tip standing open.

He wrestled the mighty moose antlers from the car roof. Staggered with them as far into the tip as he could manage, dumped them and raced back to his car.

'Thank goodness for that,' he gasped, leaping into his little yellow car. 'I thought I'd never get rid of them.'

And then he sped off, as if they might be chasing him.

*

Grandad was asking Professor Kettles, 'But what about that Little Waif? Is she still wandering about out there? Just *who* is she?'

'Her name,' the Professor said, 'is Jane Shore.'

'*She*'s Jane Shore?' said Grandad, amazed. 'I can't believe it!'

Cruncher said, 'But wasn't she that evil kid who —'

Prof Kettles silenced him with a look. 'No, she wasn't. But I'll tell you all about that later. There's no time now.'

No time either to find Claw. Cruncher had already told the Professor that his crisp-making machine had crawled off somewhere. Just a short time ago, that machine had mattered to the Prof more than anything. Even more than people. But now his priorities had changed. He hadn't thought about crackle quotients for ages.

'It's just us three,' said Prof Kettles, looking round at his little team, 'versus the Space Potato.'

'What about getting some help?' asked Grandad.

'No time,' said Prof Kettles grimly. 'We have to act now.'

Every second was vital to stop the spread of the Space Potato. It might already be too late.

'Got any crisps?' asked Cruncher, desperately. Just a bag would do. First he'd slash it open with his dagger thumb. *Rrrip!* And then –

'Oh no!' moaned Cruncher. He kept forgetting that thumbnail was gone. He was really going to miss it.

But neither Grandad nor Prof Kettles seemed to have heard him. They were too busy talking tactics.

'We'll go for the mother plant first,' said Prof Kettles. 'The problem is how to get close enough to it without being caught. And then we need some weapons . . .'

Grandad stopped frying sausages. He'd just had a brainwave.

'I know exactly what we need,' he said. 'Come and look at this.'

He dashed out of the caravan. Cruncher and Prof Kettles were hot on his heels. He was fiddling with keys. He threw open the big double doors of his top-secret shed.

'Here's the answer,' he said. 'My re-designed refuse vehicle for the Global Orbital Retrieval of Interstellar Artefacts.'

'Pardon?' said Cruncher.

'It's the posh name for cleaning up space garbage,' said Grandad. 'Just call her GLORIA, like I do.'

Cruncher groaned. 'But it's just an old bin van, Grandad. I've already seen it through the shed windows.'

'Ah, but you haven't seen her hidden features,' said Grandad. 'If Gloria could fly, she could clean up space, no problem. And if there were a whole fleet of her . . .'

'You mean, this thing can't even fly yet?' said Cruncher scornfully.

'What do you think I am?' said Grandad. 'A rocket scientist? I'm a waste disposal expert.'

Cruncher climbed up into the cab.

'Though she does have one or two rocket features,' added Grandad, as he heaved himself up after Cruncher.

Prof Kettles was already in the cab. 'Fascinating!' he said.

The driving wheel was in the centre. On either side of it were control panels, crammed with buttons, switches.

Grandad switched on Gloria's engine.

'These gadgets I've designed to trap space

junk,' said Grandad. 'They might just work with Space Potatoes.'

'It's like the starship *Enterprise*,' said Cruncher, as lights glowed and flashed on the control panel.

Grandad was right, the old bin van wasn't what she seemed. 'What's this do?' he asked Grandad, his finger hovering over a switch.

'No, no,' warned Grandad. 'Don't touch anything. Not unless I tell you. Remember Gloria is still in the experimental stage.'

Grandad began backing Gloria out of the shed.

A plummy voice filled the cab: 'This vehicle is reversing.'

'Who's that, the Queen?' said Cruncher, staring round.

'Oh that,' said Grandad. 'That's Gloria's warning voice. That was already in the van when I bought it.'

'It's very posh,' said Cruncher. 'For a bin van.'

'I like it,' said Grandad. 'It gives garbage disposal a bit of class.'

The posh voice came again. 'This vehicle is reversing. Caution, pedestrians! Caution, cyclists!'

'I don't think you'll need that in space, Grandad,' advised Cruncher.

Grandad drove. Prof Kettles and Cruncher sat on either side of him, staring out of the windscreen.

Gloria rumbled out of Grandad's Little Kingdom and through the great metal gates of the council tip.

The tip was spread before them like a dark wilderness. Strange crackles of energy chased through the gloom. The storm clouds glowed from inside, casting a spooky yellow light over the whole scene.

It was obvious something alien had taken over.

'What does this Space Potato look like, anyhow?' asked Cruncher.

'Don't you remember?' said Prof Kettles, astonished.

Cruncher had been closer to it than any of them. He'd been in its sticky grasp. Was almost drawn into its hissing heart.

But Cruncher shook his head. He couldn't remember much from when he was brain-washed. Except, except – there was a pesky little tune he kept humming. Something about potatoes. Where had that come from? Surely it wasn't from *Top of the Pops*?

'Got your seat belts on?' asked Grandad, before flipping a switch. *Vroom.* With a sudden surge of power, Gloria shot forwards.

'Caution, driver! You are exceeding the speed limit!' said the plummy voice.

'*Aaargh!*' Cruncher was flung forwards, then slammed back into his seat.

'What's that?' he asked Grandad, through rattling teeth.

'It's Gloria's rocket boosters.'

'I thought you said she couldn't fly.'

'She can't,' said Grandad. 'They just give her a little extra acceleration, that's all. Hang on!'

The old bin van lurched across the tip like a turbo-charged tank. Spurts of fire from the rocket boosters flamed behind her. Cans were crushed under her tyres. Grandad clung on grimly to the driving wheel.

And suddenly they were surrounded by garbage mountains. It was as if night had fallen. Grandad switched on the headlights. Gloria stormed through the darkness, lights and fiery tails blazing.

'There it is!' cried Prof Kettles above the engine's roar. 'The Space Potato.'

Cruncher followed his gaze. The hairs on the back of his neck wriggled. If he'd met that *thing* before, surely he would have remembered?

You couldn't see the garbage mountain it grew on. The Space Potato's snaky arms had swarmed all over it. More arms waved wildly against the sky. It seemed to be growing bigger, more powerful, almost as you watched.

A flock of swans flew over, slow and graceful between the storm clouds and the mountain tops.

Instantly, the Space Potato crouched, waiting. Cruncher hadn't seen it snatch birds before. But somehow, he knew what was going to happen.

'No!' cried Cruncher.

But the sticky arms shot out, dragged the swans down in a flurry of white feathers. Only two escaped.

'It's a monster!' said Cruncher. 'Did you see what it just did?'

'It's certainly a very unusual species,' said Prof Kettles, trying to sound calm.

He considered potatoes his friends – but

even *his* voice shook a little. This spud was a voracious and cunning predator. If they didn't stop it right now, it could wipe out the entire human race.

'Don't go any closer,' said Prof Kettles. 'Just circle the bottom of the garbage mountain.'

'Defence shields up!' said Grandad, concentrating on driving.

'What?' said Cruncher.

'That button there,' said Grandad, still staring through the windscreen.

'What, this one?' Cruncher lunged at the nearest button.

'No! That makes Gloria magnetic!'

'*Whoops*,' said Cruncher.

Instantly, metal junk rose from the tip. Tin cans, wire coat hangers, an old car battery. They hovered spookily in the air. Then were sucked towards the bin van by a strong magnetic pull. They dived on to Gloria like a flock of freaky metal birds. *Clang, clang, clang.* They stuck all over her sides and roof so she looked like a moving scrapyard. The bin van seemed to sag under the weight. Now she was limping along, at tortoise speed. Even her rocket boosters didn't help.

173

Grandad flung himself at a lever, yanked it down, broke the electro-magnetic circuit.

All the junk hitching a ride fell off. Gloria, free of her load, leapt forwards.

'Collecting space junk with a magnetized vehicle,' said Prof Kettles. 'Brilliant!'

'Course,' Grandad was saying, 'in space, the junk wouldn't slow her down. It's weightless up there, where there's no gravity and . . .'

Tap, tap, tap, tap.

Something was tapping on Gloria's side window.

Cruncher turned his head, very slowly. Saw the tip of a long, bushy tentacle.

'It's the Space Potato!' It had sneaked up on them.

It was rapping on the glass, testing its strength, trying to get in.

'I thought we were safe at the bottom of the mountain,' said Prof Kettles. 'Those stems must stretch like elastic!'

Grandad sprang into action. Pressed the button Cruncher should have pressed before. Metal grilles slid up to protect Gloria's windows. They were meant to protect her from space junk. But Space Potatoes were even more dangerous.

'*Yurgh!*' Cruncher was flung sideways as the bin van swerved. The Space Potato had vanished from the window.

'It's got a grip on the back axle!' said Grandad, fighting to control the steering. Gloria's tyres spun in the dirt, flung up clouds of mud. She rocked, jolted forwards, stopped, jolted forwards again. It was a tug of war – that tentacle had amazing strength. Gloria was winning, but only just.

But more arms were writhing down the mountain to help. Trying to find holds on the back of the bin van.

Gloria's engine rose to a shrill scream.

'Caution, driver! The engine is overheating!' protested the frightfully posh voice.

'Come on, old girl,' urged Grandad. 'I know you're tough as old boots. I need more power.'

But the rocket boosters were on full power already. Gloria gave a great shudder. 'Oh no,' said Cruncher.

She had put up a brave fight. But, they all felt it – they were sliding backwards. Being hauled up the slope by the mother plant.

'Jump!' said Prof Kettles. 'It's got us!'

'No,' said Grandad. 'Not yet.'

He hit another button. 'This'll fix it.'

A growling sound came from Gloria's rear. Grandad had started her crusher. The crusher had been specially strengthened to mangle space junk. Pulping a plant, even a super spud, should be no problem at all.

'It's working,' said Grandad.

They could see in the bin van's big wing mirrors. The ends of the thrashing arms were being minced in Gloria's great metal jaws. As if she was munching an octopus.

They were free! Grandad stomped on the accelerator. Put lots of distance between them and the Space Potato.

Grandad braked. They all peered through the window grilles back at the garbage mountain. Hissing came from the top. It swelled to a mighty roar, louder than oceans.

Prof Kettles said, 'I think we've made it angry.'

The Space Potato's sticky branches were waving wildly. It sensed humans inside the bin van. It had been thwarted once, when Cruncher had escaped its clutches. It wasn't going to let them escape again.

'If I could get close enough to that beast,'

said Grandad, 'Gloria would make mincemeat of it. Arm by arm.'

He revved up and sped towards the garbage mountain with the crusher still chomping.

Prof Kettles opened his mouth to say, 'It's too risky.'

But Gloria got in first: 'Caution! Caution!'

'You can do it, Gloria,' said Grandad, his mouth set in a grim line.

Something crashed on to Gloria's roof.

'Have you made her magnetic again?' cried Grandad.

'What me? I haven't touched anything,' said Cruncher. Another object hit the roof, bounced off. 'Anyway, it's not metal junk,' said Cruncher, 'it's a tractor tyre.'

The tyre rolled away into the tip's murky depths.

Prof Kettles stared out the window. 'It's fighting back! Throwing things at us. I told you it was a potato with brains.'

One of the space spud's arms slithered out, grabbed a rock. Yanked it out of the mud like a rotten tooth.

'Duck!' said Prof Kettles.

Its aim was deadly. The rock smashed

against the windscreen. If the grille hadn't been there, it would have shattered. An arm could have reached in, plucked them from the safety of Gloria's cab.

Cruncher shuddered. 'Don't let it get us!' he said.

Memories were coming back – of being in a green, sticky embrace; of hearing hissing right in his ear.

The bin van lurched through a hail of missiles. Every arm of the Space Potato was chucking whatever it could find. An old wardrobe smashed into the cab.

'Let's give it a taste of its own treatment!' said Grandad. 'Drive!' he ordered Prof Kettles, handing over the wheel.

He tapped keys on Gloria's control panel. 'Look in the wing mirrors,' he told Cruncher.

Two strange glittering structures, like giant-sized fairy wings, unfolded from Gloria's sides.

'So she *can* take off,' breathed Cruncher, wild with hope.

An image came into his mind. Of Gloria, soaring above the reach of the Space Potato. Breaking through the clouds into the blue beyond. Doing victory rolls while her posh voice warned, 'Caution, cyclists. This vehicle is reversing.'

'They're not wings,' said Grandad, dashing Cruncher's dreams. 'They're space junk dispersal bats – for whopping junk into low Earth orbit so it burns up.'

'But they're made of old mattress springs,' said Cruncher.

'Brilliant, isn't it?' said Grandad. 'All my inventions use stuff other folk have dumped. Course, in space, you'd have to have special, super-strong metal –'

'Watch out!' yelled Prof Kettles as the Space Potato scored more direct hits.

'You can control the bats from the cab,' continued Grandad, as if they weren't under attack. 'Someone dumped this old computer. And it was still working.'

Surely, thought Cruncher, *he isn't going to bang on about people's wastefulness now?* 'Grandad!' he begged.

Grandad jiggled a joystick on the control panel.

The left-side bat swivelled this way, that. Missed a flying rock.

'Darn!' said Grandad. 'This needs good coordination.'

'I can do it!' cried Cruncher.

'The right-hand bat's all yours.'

Cruncher crouched over his controller, watched his bat in the wing mirror. Checked for incoming missiles at the same time.

Here came another tyre, spinning towards them like a frisbee. Cruncher jiggled frantically. All those hours playing computer games weren't wasted after all.

'Got it.' He thwacked it back into the writhing heart of the Space Potato. *Sssssssss!* The monster plant cowered at the impact.

'Good shot!' said Grandad.

Cruncher allowed himself a brief grin.

Then he hunched again over the controls, concentrating, his eyes steely slits.

The huge springy bat twisted this way, that, as Cruncher lined it up with a flying rock.

'Get nearer!' said Cruncher.

'No,' Prof Kettles shook his head. 'It's too risky.'

'I'm going to mince the monster!' cried Grandad, putting the crusher on full power. He grabbed Gloria's wheel back from the Professor. 'Cruncher, you get those rocks.'

Grandad started backing Gloria up the garbage mountain.

'Caution! This vehicle is reversing.'

Suddenly Cruncher's stomach seemed to plunge down a pit.

'What's happening?'

Gloria had been lifted clean into the air. Her tyres spun, uselessly.

'I told you it was intelligent!' said Prof Kettles. 'That missile attack was just a diversion.'

The potato had been cunning. Its tentacles had slithered across the mud while they were looking up into the skies.

And now it had got them. Bushy arms wrapped Gloria up like an Egyptian mummy. There was a terrible wrenching sound. Space Potato arms tore off the space junk dispersal bats, flung them aside. Like a cruel child pulling the wings off a fly.

They crawled over the windscreen, tugging at the metal grille. Began to rip it right off. Gloria was being lifted higher.

'Abandon bin van!' yelled Grandad. He pushed Cruncher out of the cab. Cruncher dropped to the ground, his fall broken by an old mattress.

Someone grabbed the back of his coat. It was Prof Kettles. 'Run!'

All three of them slid down the slopes of rotting rubbish. Ran as fast as they could, far away from the garbage mountain. Dived for cover behind an old fridge freezer.

Cruncher stuck his head up to see what was happening.

'Gloria!' cried Grandad, in an anguished voice.

The Space Potato was hauling the bin van back up the slope to its mountain-top stronghold. Gloria's engine was still running. Her headlamp beams swivelled madly through the gloom. The rocket boosters blazed like SOS flares. 'Caution! Caution!' came a strangled voice from inside.

Prof Kettles, Grandad and Cruncher watched helplessly. They had been defeated, just like Silas Smite. The Space Potato was too powerful. Even now, it was growing more arms to replace the ones it had lost.

'We can't stop it,' said Grandad. 'No one can.'

Then, from a mountain top, a dazzling light blazed out, like a meteor.

They all recognized it at once.

'It's Jane,' said Prof Kettles, in an awed whisper.

And each of them felt a strange new feeling inside them. It bubbled, like a tiny, bright fountain. It was hope.

Jane's silver beams spread out over the council tip. Reached into even its murkiest corners. Spilled over the three of them, then over the strangling arms of the Space Potato.

Instantly, the Space Potato seemed to shrivel, like a slug sprinkled with salt. It cowered, as if it was scared.

For a few seconds, it loosed its grip on Gloria. The bin van slipped from the tentacles' grasp. Crashed back down to the garbage mountain.

The Space Potato arms raced to get it back. But they were too late.

The crusher was chewing into the garbage mountain, deeper and deeper, as if Gloria was trying to dig an escape tunnel. The bin van was half buried already. The Space Potato arms struggled to haul her out.

From the dark hole Gloria was munching came crimson flames. It was her rocket boosters still firing. You could only see her cab now. If she carried on burrowing, she'd soon be down to Robin's Corner.

Cruncher screwed up his eyes. 'Is that mountain moving? Is it an earthquake?'

The Space Potato's mountain den seemed to be heaving. The slopes were splitting open. Blue fire showed through the cracks. As if there was a rumbling volcano down there, getting ready to blow.

'Run!' shrieked Prof Kettles. 'Gloria's rocket boosters have ignited the methane gas!'

They'd just raced out the tip gates when, behind them, there was an almighty *BOOM*! Cruncher staggered about, blinded by light. The explosion rattled round his skull, took ages to fade away.

At last, there was silence.

'Look,' said Grandad, tugging Cruncher's arm.

All three of them stared. The Space Potato had gone. Even the garbage mountain wasn't there any more. It had been blown sky high. Rubbish had been scattered for miles.

Silas Smite's nostrils would have been quivering – everywhere there was a strong smell of cooking spuds. The mother Space Potato had been roasted in her jacket – then blown away. Just like all the baby spuds. In the town it was raining roast potatoes and bits of green tentacle.

'That Space Potato,' said Prof Kettles, 'has had its chips.'

He knew it had to be destroyed. But he couldn't help feeling just a hint of sadness. It was the most magnificent potato plant he'd ever seen. And now there was nothing to remind him. Not even a photo.

Grandad wasn't looking at where the garbage mountain had been. His gaze had gone higher. 'Gloria,' he gasped.

Launched out of her hole like a rocket, Gloria had blasted into the heavens trailing fiery tails.

'She's flying,' breathed Cruncher, that starry look in his eyes. 'That's beautiful.'

The explosion had scattered the storm clouds. Gloria was high up, soaring into a pure blue sky.

Then, as they watched, she suddenly stopped dead. The rocket boosters went out. So did the headlights.

'She's run out of power!' cried Prof Kettles. Both he and Cruncher braced themselves. There was nothing to stop her crashing back to Earth.

Only Grandad was smiling serenely.

Why isn't he going bananas? thought Cruncher. Soon his precious space-junk-retrieval vehicle would be in pieces on the ground.

'Watch,' said Grandad, as if he could read Cruncher's mind.

Four parachutes suddenly opened above Gloria like big, white blossoms.

'Re-entry parachutes!' marvelled Prof Kettles.

'Just another of my little rocket features,' said Grandad modestly.

The battered bin van came swinging gently down over the tip.

Don't put her down in a potato lagoon, thought Cruncher. *It's horrible in there. Like stinking mouldy old porridge.*

Why were these strange, disturbing memories suddenly surfacing? And he'd remembered something else about the potato lagoons. He saw it in his head, clear as day.

He saw Claw, doing a doggy-paddle, dragging him to the shore.

'Claw saved me,' Cruncher whispered to himself. 'That's how I got out.'

'What?' said Grandad,

'Oh, nothing,' sighed Cruncher. But his

heart was sore. The metal gauntlet had saved his life. He felt really guilty now that he'd told it to go away. How could he have been so ungrateful, so cruel?

But Claw had gone for good.

'I don't blame it,' muttered Cruncher. 'After the way I behaved.'

There was no way now that he could put things right.

The parachutes didn't dump Gloria in the potato lagoons. They carried her safely over them and landed her inside Grandad's Little Kingdom.

Prof Kettles' eyes were searching the garbage mountain where Jane had been standing. Could he still see a silver shimmer on the top?

'No, she's gone,' he sighed.

He wasn't surprised. Her job here was finished. There was no reason for her to stick around.

'What happened to her *after the fire*?' he murmured to himself. Now he would never find out.

But suddenly, as if Jane could hear him, he heard her voice in his head: 'I stowed away, on a ship to America.'

No time for details, her voice was fading. 'Did you find happiness?' asked Prof Kettles urgently, inside his head. He was desperate to know. It mattered to him more than crackle quotients, even more than making the perfect crisp.

Jane's answer was hard to catch. No more than a whisper in the wind, the faintest echo.

'She said "Yes",' Prof Kettles told himself, smiling. 'I *know* she said "Yes".'

The driver of the yellow three-wheeler had just got back to his house. He was locking the car door when there was a whistling sound right overhead. He looked up. His mouth fell open. A huge set of moose antlers came plummeting down from the sky, bounced off the roof of his tiny car and left a big dent.

Was this some kind of curse? Would he never get rid of them?

With a deep, despairing sigh, the driver wrestled them on to his car roof again. He lashed them there with rope. Then climbed into his yellow peril. And set off, for the third time that day, to the council tip.

Chapter Fifteen

Three weeks later.

Cruncher was on his way to Chapel Crisps. Professor Kettles had said, 'Come and meet Claw Two.' The Prof's new robot hand had been sent, Special Delivery, from Japan.

The crisp production line was up and running again. Chapel Crisps were back in the shops.

That should have thrilled Cruncher to bits. But, strangely, he found himself getting more and more lukewarm about the whole crisp-eating experience.

He didn't get that old buzz, even with his new, regrown dagger thumbnail.

He slashed the bag open, crammed the crisps into his mouth, *KERRUNCH*, just like before. But he couldn't recapture that cave-man feeling.

It was as if he'd had some kind of aversion therapy without knowing it. Was it anything to do with that sinister little song that ran through his head every time he saw a crisp bag and filled him with feelings of *doom*? How could it be? He couldn't even remember the words.

Cruncher was pleased he'd conquered his crisp addiction. Of course he was. After all, he was starting his new school tomorrow. And giving up crisps had been a major part of his self-improvement plan.

But, secretly, he couldn't help feeling just the tiniest twinge of regret. For the old, cosy times, when he didn't have to worry about his image. When he'd snuggled up in bed with a comic book and twenty-three bags of Chapel Crisps.

Cruncher reached the council tip. Yellow JCBs were crawling all over the garbage mountains. Bin vans were busy going in and out. It was hard to believe that three weeks ago, here on these mountains of rotting rubbish, the fate of all mankind had hung in the balance.

We'd all have been spud-hating zombies or a Space Potato's dinner if it hadn't been for Jane Shore, thought Cruncher.

Somewhere on the tip, mangled and smashed under the JCBs' wheels, were Silas Smite's pulpit and his black marble memorial stone. After the crisis was over, and the old villain had been sucked back into history, one of the first things the Prof had done was get rid of any reminders of him from the crisp factory.

But it was much harder to erase him from your brain. Cruncher shuddered. The picture of the mad, spud-hating preacher was still very fresh in his mind. Perhaps the memory would fade. But he didn't think he would ever forget.

Cruncher passed Grandad's Little Kingdom. Cruncher couldn't see him – he was probably in the big shed, tinkering with Gloria. But he planned to see him later. He had a question to ask Grandad. He'd remembered it last night when *Star Trek* came on telly. It was: 'Grandad, just what *is* the snag with Scavenger Worms?'

'OK,' said Cruncher to Prof Kettles, 'where's this new claw then?'

'It's the very latest in crisp technology,' Prof Kettles told him, proudly. 'Much faster and more efficient than the old claw.'

Cruncher walked with the Professor over to the conveyor belt. He didn't slither any more. He'd got himself a new pair of grippy trainers.

'MEET AND GREET!' said Prof Kettles. This time he didn't use an American accent but trilled the command, in a high fluty voice.

'What are you talking like that for?' asked Cruncher.

'Because this claw only responds to ladies' voices. You try. Talk like a lady.'

'No way!' said Cruncher, blushing. He had his new cool image to think about. His pink hairnet was slipping. Without thinking, he pushed it out of his eyes.

'MEET AND GREET!' twittered Prof Kettles again.

Claw Two shot up from the conveyor belt. It shook Cruncher's hand. It looked very like the old claw, a metal gauntlet. But it wasn't the same. There just wasn't the same spark. You could never imagine it flipping a finger at Prof Kettles. Or saving someone from a potato lagoon. This claw had no personality, no mind of its own. It was just a crisp-making machine, pure and simple.

Prof Kettles was pleased. 'This one won't rebel and run off,' he told Cruncher, as Claw Two obediently peeled, sliced and fried.

But Cruncher felt oddly despondent. He still hadn't forgiven himself for driving the old claw away.

Cruncher didn't even take the free crisp samples the Prof offered him. He went trailing outside. He was in a very melancholy mood. Seeing that new machine in Claw's place had started it, brought all the memories flooding back.

He was remembering how Claw had dragged itself away, hurt and rejected. How he'd called it a monster, screamed after it, 'Don't come back!'

Where was Claw now?

It won't come back here, that's for sure, thought Cruncher. *Not after what you shouted at it.*

Cruncher felt a strange sensation. Something was tugging at his trousers. He looked down.

'Claw!'

The metal gauntlet wasn't glittering now. It was grimy with dirt. It didn't look menacing –

just hunched-up and sorry for itself. Where had it been all this time?

Cruncher didn't know it, but Claw hadn't got any further than the council tip. It had been hiding there for the last three weeks. Scurrying out of the way of bin vans and dodging JCBs. Finally, battered and scared, it had come crawling back to the factory where it had been a crisp-making slave. It didn't know where else to go.

'Claw,' said Cruncher again. He could hardly believe it. 'You've come back.'

Then Cruncher started stammering, 'What I did before – shouting at you and stuff. I was scared, I didn't know. Anyway, thanks for rescuing me from the potato lagoons. And, I'm really, *really* sorry.'

Claw couldn't understand. Cruncher knew that. But he just had to apologize. He tried to keep his voice soft and gentle. He knew by now that Claw hated being yelled at.

He bent down to pat Claw, as if it was a pet dog.

Claw explored his hand, very delicately. Felt that new dagger thumbnail. Its robot brain wondered, 'Mummy Claw?'

'It's me, Cruncher,' said Cruncher. But still Claw hung back, its simple brain confused. It didn't want to be driven away again.

Cruncher felt awful. He thought, 'I've done it now. Claw hates me.'

Then, suddenly, he knew what to do. He didn't know *how* he knew. But it seemed like the most natural thing in the world.

He knelt down, opened the big knee pocket in his baggy pants. Then waited. He hardly dared breathe. It was like waiting for a timid wild bird to feed from your hand.

Claw's silver talons explored. Felt inside the pocket. Would it? *Would it?*

Yes! thought Cruncher, as Claw scurried into its nest and curled up into a silver ball.

'Welcome back, Claw,' said Cruncher.

He trudged down the street. It was hard walking. But he would soon get used to it, having a robot claw in his pants. He was thrilled to bits Claw had come back. He'd felt guilty ever since that flashback, when he'd realized Claw had saved his life.

A sneery voice scattered his thoughts.

'Hello again, pink-hairnet head.'

Aaaargh! thought Cruncher. *I forgot!*

He snatched off the hairnet. But this time, the gang of boys wasn't going to let him escape. They were circling round him like wolves. He was surrounded.

Claw came out of its den, on one of its little adventures. Its savage-looking silver talons crept up Cruncher's trousers. The red wires trailed repulsively from its wrist.

'What is it?' gibbered one of the boys, pointing.

Whirr. Click. Claw swivelled round to track the voice vibrations. Its talons reached out, like a wizard casting a spell . . .

'Run!' screamed the boys. They legged it, diving down alleys, crashing into dustbins.

Cool, thought Cruncher.

This time, he didn't need crisps to give him that caveman feeling. Help him get over the trauma of being caught in a hairnet. Because, now, he had Claw.

Cruncher wasn't expecting trouble at secondary school. Not now he'd conquered his two most embarrassing habits. But, just in case, he might take Claw along. One look at Claw was enough to make any bullies run a mile.

Just so long as they never found out that,

inside that scary metal hand, was a sensitive, touchy-feely creature who only wanted to be loved.

Chapter Sixteen

Cruncher and Claw were in Cruncher's bedroom. It was late at night. Cruncher was reading. Claw was on the carpet. The metal hand was getting bolder, like a hermit crab coming out of its shell.

Claw clicked its fingers, as if to say, 'Watch me!'

Cruncher yawned, 'What now?' Raised his eyes from his book.

Claw was juggling with Cruncher's glass marbles. The ones he'd had since he was a little kid.

'Yeah, very clever,' said Cruncher. Claw did several backflips. Then tapped out a drum solo, '*Ratatatatat,*' on Cruncher's pencil tin.

'Tuneful,' said Cruncher.

Claw galloped round the room, like a curious child, pulling Cruncher's boxer shorts out of drawers, messing up his neat collection of fantasy warriors. It seemed very happy.

But, *Phew*, thought Cruncher. *It's going to wear me out. When am I going to get some peace and quiet?*

'Go to sleep, Claw,' said Cruncher.

Did the metal gauntlet understand? Probably not. But it scuttled round the floor in circles, like a puppy having a mad half hour before bedtime. Then *click*, *whirr*, it curled into a silver ball. It seemed to be sleeping.

'At last,' said Cruncher, switching out the light.

Claw was turning out to be quite a handful.

But Cruncher grinned to himself, 'You'll have to get used to it.' A claw is for life, not just for Christmas.

Suddenly, Cruncher shot up in bed. 'I never asked Grandad!' He'd never even been to see him – he'd spent the whole day getting reacquainted with Claw. Cruncher grabbed his mobile.

He punched in Grandad's number. Mum had just brought Grandad a mobile. Had he remembered to switch it on? Yes, he had. It was ringing.

A gruff voice answered. 'Yep?'

'It's me, Grandad,' gabbled Cruncher. 'I've got to know. Just what is the snag with Scavenger Worms?'

'The snag is,' said Grandad, 'that they can't breed successfully in space. Because in space there's no gravity.'

'What difference does that make?' asked Cruncher.

There was a surprised pause from Grandad's end. When he started to talk again, he was using very simple words. 'Well, Cruncher, it's like this. If the mummy and daddy worms keep floating apart they can't make babies. I know this might come as a shock, but to make babies a mummy and daddy have to . . .'

'*Aaaargh!*' shrieked Cruncher, feeling his toes curl. He gabbled into the phone, 'Grandad! Please, please stop! I know all that stuff already!'

He switched off his mobile. *I wish I hadn't asked*, he thought. Was there *anything* about Scavenger Worms that wasn't embarrassing?

He checked Claw. The great metal hand was still curled up tight. It had worn itself out playing.

'Awwww!' smiled Cruncher, like a fond parent.

It twitched in its sleep as if it was dreaming.

What do claws dream about? wondered Cruncher.

But it was time to get some sleep himself. It was a big day tomorrow. His first day at his new school.

He switched off the light again. Dozed off. His dagger thumb slid up to his mouth. Something deep in his sleeping brain warned him: *Don't do that. You'll hurt yourself.* The dagger thumb slid down again.

But then Cruncher's left-hand thumb crept up and slid into his mouth instead.

That left-hand thumb was sneaky. It had been doing this for ages, ever since Cruncher grew his right-hand dagger thumbnail. But just before Cruncher woke up, it always slid out of his mouth again.

So that Cruncher would never suspect that, every night, it helped him sleep like a baby and have sweet dreams.

Cruncher slept peacefully on, with Claw curled up on the carpet beside his bed.

DR FELL'S CABINET OF SMELLS

Susan Gates

'Have I got this right? This Dr Fell guy saved people's smells? That's sick!'

When Kit and Juniper find themselves with the latest high-tech E-nose, they discover they can reproduce not just the smells Dr Fell saved, but actual people from the past. Suddenly they're face to face with a real gladiator, smelling of geraniums – and that's just for starters!

'Susan Gates is a truly funny children's writer' – *Independent*

Choosing a brilliant book
can be a tricky business...
but not any more

www.puffin.co.uk

The best selection of books at your fingertips

So get clicking!

Searching the site is easy – you'll find
what you're looking for at the click of a mouse,
from great authors to brilliant books and more!